Let It Burn

The Barrington Billionaires

Book Four

Ruth Cardello

Author Contact

website: RuthCardello.com
email: Minouri@aol.com
Facebook: Author Ruth Cardello
Twitter: RuthieCardello
Goodreads
goodreads.com/author/show/4820876.Ruth_Cardello
Bookbub
bookbub.com/authors/ruth-cardello

Billionaire Andrew Barrington walked away from the lavish lifestyle he was raised in to serve as a Marine. Until recently, he would have said he'd made the right choice. A tragic set of events, however, has him not reenlisting and emotionally hitting rock bottom.

Helene Franklin is visiting her uncle as part of an extended vacation in Aruba. She trades her bikini for an office job when he says there is trouble brewing at his clinic and asks her to keep an eye out for anything unusual.

Every Marine needs a mission. To appease his family, Andrew heads to Aruba to track down what he believes is a wild goose chase. Expecting to discover nothing, he meets a quirky, irresistible virgin who is just about to turn his whole world upside down.

His questions will put her in danger.

Her love will set him free.

What will they gain and what will they lose when they both decide to. . .let it burn?

Copyright

Dedication

This book is dedicated to every armed service person who has returned home carrying the weight of what they experienced.

Thank you for your service and God bless you.

You are not alone.

A Note to My Readers

I fall in love with each of my heroes as I write them, but **Andrew Barrington** *holds a special place in my heart. It could be because he's so damaged at the beginning of the book. I cried as I wrote that scene.*

No, it's more than that. I knew Andrew would be a character who always stayed with me when my husband, a retired Marine, read the opening over my shoulder then sat down beside me. It's not unusual for my husband to read my stories and make suggestions, but the first chapter moved him enough that he started sharing stories of men he'd known who came back in the same heartbreaking condition.

It was important to my husband that Andrew was portrayed in a way that honored the real struggle veterans often face when they come home. If you read a scene and tear up, know that my husband and I wrote it with tears in our eyes. If you feel yourself cheering for him to make it, know that we cheered for him, too. He became real to us.

This is a photo of my husband who retired after serving for twenty-two years. He's not afraid to come to someone's defense, but is also an incredibly kind and supportive soul.

We wrote a wild adventure for Andrew and, Helene Franklin, the woman he falls in love with. My husband and I spent about as much time laughing our butts off as we did wiping tears from our eyes. Helene is a quirky virgin with a strong sense of self, and exactly what Andrew needs.

Come fall in love with my favorite Barrington brother, Andrew.

My billionaire world at a glance:

Chapter One

>>>><<<<

A month earlier

A REPEATING LOUD noise in the distance pierced through Andrew Barrington's dreamless sleep, pulling him grudgingly back from the only part of the day he found comfort in. Lately, sleep required a substantial combination of alcohol and sleep aids. It was a dangerous game of chemical Russian roulette, and one he was beginning to think he'd rather lose.

He threw an arm out to see if he was alone. Christy, or maybe her name was Christine, had attached herself to him a couple weeks ago after they'd hooked up at a bar. She said he was not only gorgeous, but fucked up just enough for her. He didn't ask and she didn't say if she was a prostitute. In the last month, she'd tracked him down several times to spend the night with him. The next day there was always money missing from his wallet, but she was a good fuck who didn't ask questions so he hid his credit cards and padded his wallet with extra bills for her. He couldn't remember if she'd come home with him the night before or not. The days had begun to blur into each other.

Realizing the loud noise was someone knocking on his door had him cursing. "Whoever you are, go the fuck away," he snarled.

The door crashed open and a man walked across the room toward him.

What the fuck?

He closed the now damaged door behind him. "The name is Emmitt Kalling. I was hired to find you."

Andrew sat up slowly, hating how the room spun almost as much as he hated the stranger before him. "By my family?" *Only they would resort to something this dramatic.* "I'll pay you double what they paid if you say you couldn't find me."

Emmitt looked around the room at the trash and piles of clothing. He kicked a pair of women's underwear out of his way as he stepped farther into the room. "How long have you been like this?"

After rubbing a hand over his throbbing temple, Andrew swung his feet around and stood with a groan. He left Emmitt standing in the middle of his hotel room while he took a much-needed piss then caught his reflection in the mirror and curled his lip in disgust. It hadn't taken long for his outside to reflect how he felt on the inside. He leaned on his hands and looked into his bloodshot eyes. *Did I finish the Jack Daniels last night? I could use it now.*

Emmitt spoke from the doorway of the bathroom. "What the fuck happened to you?"

A flash of a memory pierced through Andrew, and he clutched the sink counter. *Her smile. Her fucking smile.* He couldn't get it out of his head. Lofton's seven-year-old, pretty-as-ever, chocolate-eyed daughter had run to him when she'd seen him, assuming her father was one step behind him. Her bright smile had filled his mouth with the taste of his own vomit. "Is your mother here, Giniya?"

"She's in the bathroom and told me not to answer the door, but I saw you in the window." She'd looked past him, not asking, but she didn't have to.

Gabrielle Lofton was quickly at her daughter's heels, but her reaction to him was much different. When she saw he was alone, she knew. Fear. Shock. Horror. Her eyes had pleaded for Andrew to deny the reason he was there. "Gini, go get a bottle of water for Uncle Andrew. I bet he's real thirsty."

"But, Mom—"

"You run along and get it, Gini. And before you come back, clean your plate from your snack."

"Is Dad—?"

"Go Gini, *now*," Gabrielle had cried, and the smile had faded from her daughter's face.

Pulling himself back from the memory, Andrew used the palms of his hands to roughly wipe at his eyes. *Fuck.* "How much is it going to take?"

Emmitt leaned on the doorjamb and shook his head. "I'm not leaving."

The anger that held him in a dark grip found an outlet. He rose to his full height. "Yes, you are."

With a shake of his head, Emmitt pushed himself off the doorframe. "Calm down, man. I don't want to hurt you."

"I'm not the one you should worry about." Andrew

turned and stepped toward Emmitt without a clear plan; all he knew was that Emmitt was leaving, one way or another. Unfortunately, the speed in which he'd turned undermined his balance and the floor came up quickly to meet him. He broke his fall with his arm and was on his knees in front of the other man, failing at first to get back to his feet. "Enjoying the show?" he growled.

"Not particularly."

"Get the fuck out of here." *No one needs to see this. Not him. Not my family.*

Emmitt crouched down in front of Andrew. "You don't need to tell me what happened, but I'm not going anywhere. I've been where you are in here." He tapped his own temple. "I've done things and seen things no man or woman ever should. There are days when I think I don't deserve to be the one who came home, but then I remember that my miserable life, insignificant as it sometimes seems to me, matters to my family. You matter to yours."

Andrew sat back on his haunches. "Was it my father? Did he send you?"

"No, Dax Marshall hired me."

"My sister's husband?"

"Yes."

"Why the hell would he? I've never met him." *I didn't even bother to go back for their wedding.*

Emmitt sighed. "He loves your sister and, by default, you. Those were his words, not mine."

Andrew closed his eyes. *He's good to her. She's always leaving me messages about how happy she is with him.* "My whole family is so fucking happy lately." *They're all getting married, having kids . . .*

"And you're here."

Andrew pushed himself back to his feet. "Exactly." He met Emmitt's eyes and said harshly, "Go back and tell them whatever will make them stop looking for me. I've got some things to work out before I can see them."

"Your brother Lance was afraid he got you killed. He was beating himself up over telling you about Aruba."

"Aruba?"

"He asked you to look into something he'd discovered over there."

Nodding tiredly, Andrew pushed past Emmitt and began to search for whatever alcohol might be left in the room. "Oh, yes, his conspiracy theory. Doctors dying. People missing. All during the same time my brother and sister were born there, twenty-nine years ago. Who gives a shit about anything that happened back then?"

"Apparently Lance does. He thinks it might have been tied to the stillborn death of Kent. Negligence that was covered up."

Andrew scored a half-full bottle of Scotch from beneath a pizza box, opened it, and took a long drink. "What does he want to do? Sue the hospital if he finds they were at fault?" *As if my family needs more money?*

Emmitt folded his arms across his chest. "He wants answers. Consider finding them for him."

After taking another long drink, Andrew wiped his mouth with his forearm. "Why would I do that?"

"Because men like you need a mission. You stay here, you'll kill yourself slowly or choose a quicker way out. You know it, and I know it. You don't want to see your family, but do you love them?"

The bottle shook in Andrew's hand. "Of course I do."

"If you give up now you pass your pain along to them. Is that what you want to do?"

His eyes filled with tears again. "No."

"Then put down that fucking drink and let me help you."

HELENE FRANKLIN BRUSHED sand from the bottom of her bare feet before stepping into the guesthouse of her uncle's Aruba home. She laid her beach bag beside the door and smiled as she closed the door. *Another day in paradise.*

Looking back, she couldn't believe she'd originally resisted making a trip to meet her mother's brother into a vacation. Until now, she'd only known Uncle Clarence through phone calls and the presents he sent for her birthday and the holidays. Meeting him hadn't felt as important as continuing to do what she'd always done: help her parents maintain their large exotic animal rescue in Florida.

She took a moment to send her parents a mental thanks for pushing her to go. Her uncle, much like the island he'd made his home, was a million times more amazing than she had ever imagined. He ran a large private clinic on Aruba and his generosity with community programs had made him a celebrity of sorts. When people found out who she was, they always had something good to say about him. He'd touched the lives of many in the small island community. Some referred to him by his local Dutch nickname, Weldoener. Translation: Benefactor. It fit him perfectly. He'd devoted his life and finances to improving the health of the people of Aruba. No one was ever turned away from his clinic. She had no idea how he continually made a profit while giving so much money away, but there wasn't any part of his story she didn't love.

The phone on the hallway wall rang. She glanced at the clock on the table and rushed to answer it. "On my way. I'll take the world's quickest shower and be right over."

"Did you even leave the beach today?" he asked in amusement.

"I didn't," she admitted without guilt. Her parents had called this her long-overdue vacation, and her uncle had told her that her presence brought him joy. Pending life decisions had been temporarily pushed to the background as she'd indulged in a few weeks of heaven.

"Don't rush. I'll have the cook keep it warm until you're ready. Call when you're walking over."

Always understanding, her uncle was simply the nicest man she'd ever met, and she hoped one day she could do something to repay his kindness. "Twenty minutes tops, I promise. I feel awful that you're waiting on me."

He chuckled. "Always so serious. You remind me of your mother. I wish she'd been able to come with you."

"Me, too. You know how she is about the rescue, though."

"Yes. I'm the same about my clinic, so I have little room

to judge her. I can't tell you how many times I've thought about going to see her, but there's always something here that needs my attention."

"And you think I'm the one who sounds like my mother?"

He chuckled again. "Take your time, little one. I have calls to answer that will keep me occupied."

Helene stopped halfway through promising again that she'd rush, laughed at herself, and hung up. He was right; she took everything too seriously. She'd heard as much from her friends her whole life. They'd usually been referring to how she chose to go home right after school each day to clean out cages and work with the animals. She'd never fully convinced them that rehabilitating animals that had frequently been illegally captured and working with organizations to return them to the wild brought her more joy than shopping, movie theaters, or school dances ever could.

After sprinting up the stairs, Helene sang her way through a quick shower and was still humming as she chose a light summer dress for dinner. She caught her reflection in the mirror and smiled. Her cheeks had a pleasant honey-tanned glow. She usually wore her hair pulled back in a practical ponytail, but here on the island she left it mostly down and thought it made her look younger.

I'm not old, but I'm definitely looking better since I've been here.

She applied a light amount of makeup, not for the benefit of her uncle, but because she felt beautiful for the first time in her life. She sniffed the material of her dress. *Maybe because I don't smell like someone who just cleaned up rhino dung?*

Not that I mind the smell. She grimaced. *I can see, though, how it might have contributed to my limited dating experience.*

Her smile faded somewhat as she remembered one of the conversations that had led to her agreeing to this trip. Her mother and father had requested a "family meeting." Her stomach had churned nervously as she'd waited for them to tell her why. The last family meeting had been when she was eighteen. Her parents had announced a loss of funding that had made it necessary for them to let go of the few employees they had. Helene had already been accepted to the University of Florida and had been excited to start classes to become a veterinarian. That dream had come to a skidding halt when her parents had explained they couldn't afford to run the rescue without her help.

Save animals in the short-run or save them in the long-run. It hadn't been an easy choice to make, but she hadn't regretted deciding to stay with her parents. Every animal they sent back, every release day photo Helene received, was a reminder that she'd made the right choice. As she'd waited for her parents to speak, she'd prayed she wouldn't hear that the future of the rescue was in danger again.

Her mother had taken her father's hand in hers, and she knew that look. The one that wondered why she wasn't out dating, why she was still single. *Here we go.* "Your father and I are worried about you."

"Why?"

"You're twenty-six, Lenny, and . . . well, we've never seen you with a man," her father said, looking as if it was as awkward for him to say as it was for her to hear.

Her mother added gently, "We want you to know that we love however God made you."

"I don't understand."

Her father had cleared his throat. "Whatever your lifestyle is, you don't have to hide it from us."

"I don't have a lifestyle," Helene had said slowly, then her eyes had rounded as she'd realized what her parents thought. "I don't have a *lifestyle*."

Her parents had exchanged a look. "I told you," her mother said.

Her father had frowned. "Pairing up is a natural part of life, Lenny. Do you have any questions about how it happens?"

There were few moments in Helene's life that could rival how mortifying being offered the *sex talk* at twenty-six had been. "Please. This is not necessary. I know how it works. I mean, I've been watching animals procreate since I was in diapers." That had sounded strange even to her own ears so she added, "Not that I watch. I just mean that I've accidentally come across animals—" She stopped there. "I don't want to have this conversation."

Her mother had shot her father a sad look. "Honey, your dad and I think you need to go out into the world for a little while. This rescue was our dream, not yours."

"I love it here," Helene had protested.

Her father had shaken his head. "You can't know that

until you've compared it to somewhere else. We were selfish. We shouldn't have let you choose keeping *our* dream over *your* dream for college. Your friends have moved on. They travel. Some are married. Nothing has changed for you except your phone rings less and less."

"I'm happy here."

"No," her mother said quietly, "you feel safe here, but Lenny, there's a whole big world out there you've never seen. I've spoken to my brother in Aruba, and he said he has a guesthouse you could stay in for a while. You've never taken a real vacation, and he knows a lot of people. Worst case, you come back with a beautiful tan and are able to tell me all about how my brother is doing. Best case, you discover your dream."

"This *is* my dream," Helene had insisted. "And you need me."

"We're doing well enough to hire a couple people. Go, Lenny. Find yourself."

"I'm not lost."

"You're going," her father had said.

It had taken a while for her to adjust to the idea of leaving the rescue, but once she had, the trip had begun to feel like an adventure rather than a shove out the door. *I am the luckiest daughter in the world to have parents like them.* Helene turned away from the mirror and practically skipped down the stairs. *I needed this.* She couldn't imagine a lifetime of doing nothing, but her weeks on the island had been good for her. At first she'd missed her parents and the rescue so much she'd been unable to enjoy herself, but that feeling had been replaced with euphoria. *I can go back to school and get my degree if I want. I can finally become a veterinarian. My parents were right, it's time to find myself.*

Helene knocked twice on the door of her uncle's mansion before letting herself in, beating the staff. They smiled at her indulgently.

Her uncle's home office door opened, and he gave her the same look. "You didn't call."

She wrinkled her nose. "Oh, my God, I forgot. I'm so sorry. I was thinking about how grateful I am to be here, and everything else fell right out of my head."

He gave her a brief hug. "I suppose that's as good of an excuse as any. Come, let's eat."

They sat across from each other at one end of a table long enough to seat twenty people. As it always did, a bounty of food and beverages appeared, delivered discretely by staff who seemed to magically disappear when not needed. Her uncle asked her about her day and listened with a smile as she described the absolute joy of hours on his private beach.

"Stop before you make me feel guilty for asking you for a favor."

"Are you kidding, Uncle Clarence? If there is some way I can repay you for three of the best weeks of my life, just say it. I'll do anything."

He gave her hand a gentle pat. "You're a good girl, Helene."

The expression in his eyes had Helene asking, "Is something wrong?"

"Nothing too serious." He took a sip of his wine. "I've

been having trouble with something at the clinic."

"What kind of trouble?"

"It's a small island and my clinic competes with the main hospital. Competition in a market like this is not always appreciated."

Helene's mouth rounded, and she leaned forward to grip his hand. "Count me in for whatever you need."

His smile returned. "Shouldn't you wait until you know what I need?"

"Uncle Clarence, you do so much for other people—you've done so much for me—it would be my honor to help."

"Politics, especially here, can be tricky to navigate. Someone is trying to dig up any mistake anyone at my clinic has ever made to try to smear my reputation. They've gone as far as to bribe people in my records department. They didn't find anything."

"Because there's nothing to find," Helene said adamantly.

He pressed his lips together briefly then said, "When someone wants to find dirt, they'll keep digging until they either find some or find something they can twist into what they want. I need someone in my records office that I trust. Someone who can't be bought."

"And that's what you want me to do? Run your records office?" The idea of clerical work when all of her experience had been manual in nature was daunting, but she knew she was up to the challenge. "What I don't know how to do, I'm sure I can learn."

"You would simply be my eyes and ears; how well you file is irrelevant. Do what you can while you're there, and who knows, maybe you'll decide you like working in an office."

She rushed around the table to give him a hug. He could dress it up however he wanted, but she didn't believe he actually needed her at the clinic. Like her parents, he was nudging her on her way. It wouldn't hurt to put some time in at the clinic before getting back on the path toward animal medicine. *Who knows? I may end up wanting to treat people. Sure I'm starting late, but my uncle's career took off later in his life. He is living proof that anything is possible.*

"When do I start?" she asked, giving him a tight squeeze.

He laughed and gave her shoulder a pat. "How about tomorrow?"

"Perfect," she said with a huge grin and returned to her seat.

And it was perfect. Not only was she in paradise, but she'd found a way to repay the person who'd made it possible for her to be there. What was better than that?

Chapter Two

Present Day

THERE WAS NOTHING sinister about the bold glass façade of Stiles Clinic. Rather than mimicking the unassuming white and blue architecture of the island's hospital, the clinic looked as if it could be dropped on Malibu Beach. Dressed in a white collared shirt and tan slacks, Andrew sat on a bench across the street from the clinic and blended in with the combination of tourists and natives meandering past. He held his phone in front of himself as if reading texts, but his attention remained focused on the building before him.

He could have charged into the building and asked to see someone in the records department, but his years as a scout sniper taught him patience and the value of reconnaissance. After watching the place for several days, he was confident that nothing out of the ordinary was happening there, at least not that week. He still wasn't sold on the benefit of being there at all, but it was better than what he'd been doing a month ago.

Thankfully, Emmitt had acted as a buffer between him and his family since then. The man's ability to lie convincingly when necessary was impressive. *Covert special assignments?* Genius. The last month, according to Emmitt, Andrew had gone through a debriefing and then a series of classified training programs that required radio silence on all sides.

Emmitt hadn't completely lied. Andrew had been in training, but it was not government sponsored. The first week had been a hellish detox in which Andrew had cursed Emmitt daily. What kept Andrew working with him, however, had been Emmitt's loyalty to not only him but the Marines in general. He'd done enough time in the Corps to understand what Andrew had faced when he left.

"You replaced one addiction with another, Andrew. What we're going to do is get you your old addiction back," Emmitt had said after the worst of the detox was over.

"I'm not an addict."

"Yes, you are. All Marines are to some extent. Before you came home, you ran three to five miles every day. You hit the gym almost as much. Natural endorphins are a type of high. You feel like shit right now, not only because you've got shit up here," he'd pointed to his own head, "but also your body is missing those endorphins. You've got nothing making you feel good. So starting today, we're running."

Every cell in Andrew's body had screamed no, but he'd said, "Bring it."

"A week from now, you'll be running again with a fifty-pound rucksack."

"Sure," Andrew had said, not completely able to imagine that happening when he still felt like road kill.

"You'll do it every day until you can't start your day without that run."

When Andrew hadn't immediately answered, Emmitt had added, "And I'll be right there kicking your ass until that happens."

That had brought a faint smile to Andrew's lips. "Someone must be paying you well."

"They paid me to find you, not do this shit. I could fly home now and still get paid."

"Then go."

"I will, as soon as your sorry ass is running a 5K without me."

His steadfast determination reminded Andrew of what a platoon sergeant had said to him when he was sent on his first deployment. "I know all about your rich family and your fancy upbringing. None of that matters here. Look at the man next to you. You'd better be ready to give your life for him. I don't give a shit what you came from or who you were before. You're a Marine now, boy. A fraud can't hide in combat." It meant that bullets didn't play favorites and money couldn't buy courage, and *that* had been a challenge Andrew had embraced. *Needed.* Loyalty and character mattered. Money made people weak, and Andrew had grown up around an abundance of it. He'd turned his back on that life, though, and enlisted in the Marines as soon as he was old enough then spent every day proving he belonged there. His greatest fear in the beginning had been turning out like his father.

Although Dale Barrington was generally liked by all, Andrew had lost respect for him early on. When trouble had come to the family, Dale had chosen to leave politics rather than fight for his career. His infidelity had shaken the family, and Andrew had never forgiven his father for it. His mother, sweet as she'd always been, was fragile and unstable. The Corps was the family Andrew had identified with. He normally kept his visits home to a bare minimum. The less involved he was with his family's drama, the simpler his life remained.

I didn't turn out like Dad; I became someone worse.

So why am I here?

Because there is nothing else on my calendar and . . . I did feel lost without a mission. This gives me something to do. After Andrew had surfaced from his "classified operations," he'd told Lance he was heading to Aruba to get the answers his brothers were looking for. Although Andrew had lacked interest in his deceased aunt's journal, he'd read it. He'd also read over the file Lance had sent him that included ramblings from a private investigator.

Yes, doctors and nurses who had worked at the clinic twenty-nine years ago were no longer there. *Big deal. Wouldn't the same be true of any clinic nearly thirty years later?*

The glass door of the clinic opened and Andrew lowered his phone to indulge in a part of his day he'd started looking forward to. A petite brunette in a conservative blue skirt and blouse strolled to the same picnic table she ate her lunch at each day. She was pretty in a wholesome, someone's little sister kind of way. Her hair always blew wildly in her face, but that never seemed to bother her. She turned her face upward and closed her eyes briefly as if receiving a kiss from the sun.

Her killer body was chastely concealed from his view, but that didn't stop him from imagining his hands gripping that perfect little ass of hers as he thrust into her. She had naturally full lips that she chewed while she opened each container of her lunch. It was a move that never failed to bring him to an uncomfortable level of arousal as he pictured exactly how good those lips would feel on him: trailing kisses down his stomach, wrapped around his cock, or parted while she cried out his name in climax.

At any other time in his life he would have acted on his attraction to her, but he wasn't himself yet. Yes, his body was back in shape. Yes, he'd replaced alcohol with a long run each day, but all it did was take the edge off. His head wasn't in a better place than it had been a month earlier. If a woman came to him he didn't turn her away, but he didn't pretend to be anything he wasn't. A good fuck could clear the mind temporarily, but he wasn't looking for conversation before or afterward. Some women were okay with that. He had a feeling that little brunette would not be.

As she always did, she took out her phone and called someone who put a sweet smile on her face. If there'd been a way to sit closer and hear her voice he would have, but instead he read her lips and imagined.

Slowly, he was getting to know her. He would have bet his life the person on the other line wasn't a man or, if it was, it wasn't someone she was dating. Nothing about her body language or what he was able to catch of their conversations was flirtatious. She laughed and munched on her lunch, all the while telling the other person about her day. He didn't understand why learning to use a computer system made her as happy as it seemed to, but he allowed himself this one distraction. He'd been watching the building for several days, and she was the most interesting person he'd seen go in or out of it—and not because she might have anything to do with his brother's conspiracy theory. She was too young for that.

The door of the building opened again, this time for a tall thin man who scanned the area before spotting the brunette and heading toward her. Andrew's eyes narrowed behind his sunglasses. He didn't like the predatory smile on the other man's face.

The man walked up and said something that surprised the brunette. She jumped and dropped her phone during her scramble to stand. He steadied her by taking hold of one of her arms, and the brunette blushed. Andrew's hand fisted beside him, and he reminded himself that she was nothing to him.

She asked the man to join her, and Andrew growled when the man did. Without knowing a thing about the tall man, Andrew didn't like him. He didn't like the way he leaned in and touched her as he spoke. He didn't like the shy smile she beamed at him.

Fuck, she's pretty when she smiles.

Like a shark circling its target, Andrew knew the man sensed her innocence and was moving in to relieve her of it. He was too smooth. Too cocky. That man would suck the life right out of her before moving on to his next conquest.

The tall man made a show of looking at his watch then leaned forward and said something to her that made her eyes widen with surprise before she nodded. She was still smiling after he left, then she looked down at her feet and saw her phone. Her laugh rang out across the distance. He watched her lips closely, willing her to keep facing him so he wouldn't miss a word.

"Did you hear that? Dr. Gunder just asked me out. Yes, a doctor. I love working here. I'm meeting so many incredible people. We're going out tonight. I will. I promise. I'm sure we won't be out late."

She rolled her eyes skyward before adding, "Don't worry, Mom. This isn't my first date." She made a face. "Wendy's cousin. I went on a date with him. And then there was—can we not get into this? Let me enjoy the fact that a doctor just asked me out." He missed a few words when she turned her face away, but she turned back a moment later. "I know what condoms are. Don't worry. I'm not going to do anything stupid."

Andrew sat forward in the bench, positive he must have lip read wrong. She sounded years younger than she looked. How innocent was she? *No. She can't be. She's in her twenties.* He shook his head.

"Now I'm sorry I told you, Mom. Don't say anything to Dad. Of course I'm talking about the date. You didn't tell him about the other thing, did you? Oh, God. Great. The two of you are giving me a complex. I know you just want me to be happy, but I am. Virginity is not a disease; I'm simply waiting for the right person."

Andrew sat back on the bench and gave his bulging cock a firm lecture. *This changes nothing.*

It did, though. The recon part of the mission was done. It'd be a cold day in hell before Andrew sat and listened to his brunette describe doing anything with the lanky doctor. The thought made his stomach clench with possessive jealousy. He rose to his feet.

What's wrong? I think he's not good enough for her?

Do I think she'd be better with someone like me?

He strode toward the front of the building. She looked up, and her eyes followed him. He shook his head. *Oh, honey, stick with your pasty doctor. He's a much safer option.*

With that, he walked into the clinic and asked if he could speak to someone in the records department. It was time to get some answers and move on.

HELENE FANNED HER face with a hand after Mr. Muscles disappeared into the clinic entrance. He carried himself like an adult male animal who'd been born in the wild. To the novice eye, all lions in captivity looked the same, but there was a distinct difference between those who had been bottle-fed by humans and those who had taken down gazelles in the Serengeti. A wild lion not only had battle scars, there was also defiance in his gait. He could be caged or even shackled, but neither made him less dangerous. He'd fought and won against animals ten times his size. He feared nothing.

Mr. Muscles was definitely wild.

By comparison, Gil Gunder reminded her of a flamingo.

The thought made Helene chuckle and chastise herself for thinking unkindly of a man she'd just agreed to go on a date with. *What's wrong with a brilliant, tall bird?*

What would I have in common with Mr. Take My Breath Away?

At best, I'd be a speed bump on his way to another hunt.

Gil is a doctor, and I want to be a veterinarian. We'll have a lot to talk about.

I wouldn't even know what to say to Mr. Muscles.

Hi, you're beautiful. Can I touch you?

That's it.

That's all I'd have.

Placing the uneaten portion of her lunch into her bag, Helene remembered her mother was still on the phone. "Sorry, Mom, I have to get back to work now."

"Call me tomorrow. And make sure you tell your uncle where you're going tonight. I'm sure if the doctor works for him, he's fine, but you can never be too careful."

She hung up, but thought: *You can be too careful.* She walked back into the clinic and down the long hallway that led to the records office. *You can be so careful that you turn around and you're a twenty-six-year-old virgin.*

Helene came to a skidding stop when she recognized the derriere of the man standing outside the door to her office. Her mouth went dry with nerves as she forced herself to approach him. "Can I . . . May I help—?"

He turned and her question fell right out of her head. Up close he was even more impressive. The curl of his lips said he knew it, too. "I'm looking for the records department."

"I'm that. The department. I'm her. She's me." She took a deep breath. "I work in that office."

"Then you're the person I'm looking for," he said with a sexy smile that made her thighs quiver. She sighed audibly when his strong hand closed around hers. "Andrew Smith."

His voice was deep and rough, matching her earlier assessment of him. Although he was dressed in casual business attire, he filled out his clothing in a way few men did. The cotton material clung to his chiseled chest just enough to highlight the breadth of it. The short sleeves were stretched to accommodate biceps so firm Helene was tempted to give one a squeeze with her free hand. A hint of a tattoo showed at the edge of one of his sleeves. She wanted to uncover it, hell uncover all of him.

"And your name?" he asked, still holding her hand.

"Me?" She swallowed hard and blinked a few times. "My name is Helene Franklin."

"It's nice to meet you."

Yes. Yes, it is. Helene shook her head and pulled her hand free. "Is there something I can do for you?"

"I hope so." The way he said those three words sent a searing heat straight through her. Her body didn't care that she didn't know him; it hummed for him.

He leaned in, and she swayed closer. "Most of the staff is out on training today, but I should be able to help you," she said.

"Good."

The only orgasms she'd had up to that point were ones

she'd brought herself, but she couldn't help but crave knowing how good things could be with a man who made her that excited simply by standing next to her.

Stop. For all I know he's awful in bed.

This is nothing more than pheromones. We're mammals at the end of the day. What I'm feeling for him is Mother Nature's way of acknowledging that he's a healthy male in his prime, and I'm still within prime mating age.

"What kind of records do you need?" Her voice was husky and revealed enough of what she was thinking to light a spark of real interest in his eyes. His nostrils flared, and she shivered when he breathed in the scent of her. "I'll give you a form to fill out. We can send the information directly to your insurance company."

"That won't be necessary. The information I'm looking for is merely to appease a curiosity. What can you tell me about a woman named Pamela Thorsen? She worked here twenty-nine years ago. Would you be able to tell me if she gave a forwarding address or a reason for leaving?"

His question was like a bucket of ice being thrown over her revving libido. "Who did you say you were?"

"Andrew Smith."

"I'm sorry, Mr. Smith, I'm not allowed to give out personal information regarding employees, present or past."

"I'm sure you can make one exception." He raised a hand and tucked one of her curls behind her ear in a tender move that would have sent her heart beating wildly if adrenaline hadn't rushed in at his earlier question. Could this man be the one who was trying to get dirt on her uncle?

"I cannot, but I would like to see your ID." The stillness that settled over him tore through her haze of attraction. She held her breath and waited.

"Why would I need to show you anything if you've already said there's nothing you can do for me?" He leaned closer still, until his mouth hovered an inch above hers. "Unless there's some way I could change your mind?"

All sorts of wonderfully filthy ideas of how he could try momentarily hampered her ability to speak. His breath caressed her lips. Clinging to her last bit of sanity, she whispered, "No, and if you don't leave I will call security."

Looking amused by the threat, he asked, "Do you call them about everyone who asks a question, or is there something about me that scares you?"

She licked her bottom lip. "Why would I be afraid of you?"

"Exactly," he purred, once again reminding her of the big cats back home. They, too, could lure a person into believing they could be trusted. Forgetting even for a moment the nature of a beast was how people got hurt.

Summoning strength, Helene held his gaze. "This department does not give out personal information about employees or patients. It's the law. If you're not sure if your question can be answered by us, you're welcome to fill out a form and we'll review your request."

He raised his head and smiled. "What if my question is about you? Should I still fill out the form?"

Even that slight withdrawal was a reprieve that allowed her to gather her thoughts. "I suppose it would depend on the question."

If he asks me out, I have to say no.

Don't I?

"What are you doing tonight?"

Oh, God. Oh, God. Oh, God. "I have a date."

"Break it."

Yes. Yes. Yes.

No. No. No.

"Why would I do that?"

"Because you deserve better than the self-absorbed sliver of a man I saw you talking to."

She searched his face and shuddered. "You were watching us?"

"I was outside and saw him with you. Trust me, once he fucks you, he'll quickly move on to someone else."

She let out a harsh breath. "Maybe that's how you operate, but he's a doctor. They take a vow to honor the well-being of people." Her hands went to her hips. "Plus, there's no need to be crass."

"Crass or honest?"

She waved a finger at him. "Either. I didn't ask for your opinion."

He raised his hands in mock surrender. "Just trying to save you from making a huge mistake. He's not the one you're waiting for." He leaned in and grazed his lips across her parted lips. "Unfortunately, neither am I."

The surprise of his kiss was followed by a surge of desire that had her kissing him back, even if only for a second before sanity returned. Lust battled with embarrassment and finally lost. She pushed him away. "Get out of my office."

"We're in the hallway."

Bringing her hand up to her mouth, she backed away from him to the door of her office and fumbled to open it behind her. "I'm calling security."

"No need. I'm leaving."

She was still clutching the doorknob. *He's not really into me. Uncle Clarence said that whoever was trying to set him up had gone as far as bribing people. What's a little flirtation compared to that? This is nothing more than an attempt to confuse me into saying something he can use against my uncle.*

She glared at him as a second possibility occurred to her. *Or he heard what I said to my mother and decided to amuse himself by taunting the oldest virgin on the planet.* Either way, he needed to know she wasn't playing along. "And don't come back. Whatever you're looking for, you won't find it here."

"That's what I keep telling myself," he said with a slanted smile before turning to walk away. Just before he turned the corner, he stopped and met her eyes over his shoulder. "Don't give yourself to that douche."

"I could sleep with everyone in this clinic, and it would be none of your business," Helene called out, but he'd already rounded the corner.

"Should I come back later?" Tina, the department's intern, asked timidly, while clutching a stack of folders to her chest.

Fighting the desire to slam the door shut and pretend Tina wasn't there, Helene forced a smile. "No. Come in. I was just practicing a line from a play I might audition for."

"Oh, okay," Tina said with a nervous laugh. "I figured it was something like that. I mean, otherwise, who would run around yelling that?"

Helene flopped into the chair behind her desk and patted an area where she wanted Tina to place the pile of folders. "Only someone who'd completely lost their mind." *Or someone who just realizes there actually is something worse than getting sex advice from one's parents: getting it from Mr. Muscles. Not only is it embarrassing, but there is that added dash of frustrated disappointment.*

I'm glad he didn't ask me out because it saves me the trouble of having to turn him down.

She covered her face with her hands. *And if I don't want people to have an opinion about my sex life, I should probably stop talking about it where they can hear.*

She looked up and noticed Tina was still watching her, no longer looking as if she believed her story.

Freakishly old virgin or clinic whore.

Which reputation would be worse?

She straightened her shoulders and asked Tina to go retrieve more files from the nursing station. *Of course, there's always a chance Tina won't say anything to anyone.*

Chapter Three

ANDREW THANKED HIS waitress for delivering a second glass of water before he'd even asked for a refill. The small, dockside seafood restaurant was a welcome reprieve from the tourist-filled hotel where he was staying. It was a local place, nothing fancy and off the beaten path enough to not be a hit with the young partiers or the blissful honeymooners. He'd eaten there the past three evenings.

Some of the waitstaff had begun hovering and talking to him about everything and nothing. They either liked the way he looked, the size of the tips he left them, or everyone on the island was just that naturally friendly. When Andrew had arrived that evening, the restaurant's owner had come out to talk to him. He'd proudly described how boats pulled up to their dock each day and sold their catch straight to the restaurant. He'd said in his soul he was a sailor, but he'd fallen in love with a woman who preferred land. The restaurant was his compromise. Andrew could see that. The balcony extended out over the water like a dare to the ocean waves. They'd talked about business and boats for a while before the man had gone back into the kitchen, but their conversation had left Andrew relaxed and in no rush to leave.

He wasn't looking forward to the next day. He'd scheduled a meeting with the private investigator his brother had hired but had nothing to tell him. If his instincts were right, that would be a theme for both of them. The death of Kenzi's twin, Kent, had nearly destroyed his family, but that didn't make it anyone's fault. His mother had traveled during the last trimester of her pregnancy with twins on assurances from her obstetrician that it was safe. She'd gone into labor, had the twins prematurely, and one hadn't survived. Tragic. Awful.

Just like life in general, it doesn't make sense at all. If life were fair I would have been the one who died.

I should have been.

No wife. No kids. Family I avoid whenever possible. I have nothing to come home to.

The pretty young hostess came to stand beside his table and balanced a menu on her hip. "You can tell me it's none of my business, but I'm so curious. Are you on vacation?"

"Not exactly."

She gave him a sweet, but suggestive, smile. "A man of few words. I like that. Are you married?"

He looked her over once. "How old are you?"

"Twenty-one."

"I'm a good ten years older than you."

"Age is just a number," she said with overblown confidence and arched her back to accentuate her large chest. The wink she shot him said she wasn't as innocent as his little brunette, but she was still too young.

He crooked a finger so she would bend closer. As she did, the front of her shirt gaped open, allowing him the intimate show that had been his goal. "You like me?"

"Yes," she said softly.

"Want to meet me after your shift?"

Her eyes widened, and her cheeks flushed. "Yes."

"Don't," he growled. "You don't know me. You don't know where I came from or what I might have done. You think I won't hurt you? Why? Because you like my face? You're too young to realize this, so let me tell you how dangerous people can be. Some hurt people for the thrill of it. You leave here with the wrong person, maybe you're dead—maybe you wish you were. Either way, in the end, it'll be on you because it was your fucking lack of good judgment that brought it on."

She recoiled and disappeared into the back of the restaurant. She must have said something to the waitstaff because they were all watching him with a combination of fear and disgust. He went back to eating, unbothered by their response.

A familiar laugh raised his attention from his plate. His hand clenched on his fork when he realized the date he'd been trying to keep out of his head all evening was about to happen a few tables away from him.

Helene Franklin and her stork of a date didn't notice him when they first took their seats. She was conservative perfection in her casual shirt and cotton slacks. The doctor was sickeningly slick in his expensive suit that was as pretentious as his oiled-back hair. There were people who had money and people who wanted everyone to think they had it. Her doctor was definitely the latter.

Andrew raised a hand to call his waitress and wasn't surprised when she made a face at him rather than come to his table. The action did, however, catch Helene's attention. Her adorable mouth dropped open when she saw him.

The doctor turned to see who she was looking at and frowned when Andrew waved. Turning back to Helene, the doctor asked who he was. She glared at Andrew briefly then dismissed him with a wave of her hand.

His view of them was temporarily blocked by the arrival of his waitress. "I wouldn't come back here if I were you. You're lucky we didn't call the police."

He met the woman's eyes as he took out his wallet. She was in her thirties or forties and appeared a lot less impressed with him than the hostess had been. "Because I was honest with her?"

"No, because you either think it's funny to scare young women or that rape is the victim's fault. Either way, you're a sick bastard."

You're right about the last part, but that's it. "My sister went with a stranger, and it didn't work out well for her. I can't stomach the idea of that young woman thinking she can trust any single man who comes in here. One day it won't go well for her, either. If scaring her into being a little more careful is wrong—then fuck being politically correct."

The expression on the older woman's face softened. "I'm sorry to hear about your sister."

"Shit happens. I just hate to see it happen needlessly.

Someone had to tell that little girl that life is brutal and fucking unforgiving. All it takes is one mistake to make you wonder if it's worth being here at all."

The sympathy in the woman's eyes made Andrew regret having said anything to her. He didn't want her pity. He didn't want anything from her or anyone else. He slapped his credit card down on the bill and looked across at Helene resentfully.

If she wants to give herself to that douche, that's her choice.
I don't care.

The waitress picked up the bill without taking the card. "My husband and I own this restaurant, and the *little girl* you scared tonight is my niece. She's given her mother plenty of grief lately. I don't like what you said to her, but I understand why you said it. Your meal is on us tonight and tomorrow night if you decide to come back. I don't know what you've been through, but being here is always worth it." She wrote a number down on his napkin. "That's my husband's number. If you need to talk to someone, he's a good listener."

"I didn't mean to sound like—"

She touched his arm gently and held out the napkin to him. "My mama always said that the world is full of some people so good they'll make you want to pray and some so bad they'll make you question if there's anyone to pray to. The trick is to fill your life with so many of the good ones that you can survive as many bastards as life sends your way."

Andrew nodded with a slight smile of appreciation. "Your mama sounds like a wise woman."

"She was. She would have paddled both of us for swearing, but then she would have hugged us and told us everything was going to be all right. It *will* be all right. Whatever happened to you, you'll get through it."

He pocketed the paper napkin. "That's what I hear."

She touched his arm again. "Come back tomorrow night and we'll make you my mama's favorite satay."

He nodded, but he couldn't imagine enjoying the restaurant again. As he stood, his gaze returned to Helene. The smile was gone from her face. Her date had moved his chair closer to hers, and while Andrew watched, she pushed the man's hand off her twice.

She was smiling nervously and shaking her head.

Andrew groaned.

He walked up to their table and bent to speak softly in the doctor's ear. "Get the hell out of here."

"I will do no such thing. Who do you think you are?" the doctor asked indignantly as he rose from his chair.

Andrew gripped the man's shoulder and shoved him back into his seat. "I'm giving you a chance to leave with your face still intact."

"I'm not going anywhere." The man looked around in desperation.

This is going to take a more personal approach. "You're on a date with my girlfriend. She likes to make me jealous. It turns her on, so I let her do it, but I don't like the way you were touching her. You should leave now before I beat the shit out of you in front of all these people."

The doctor revealed his cowardice when he turned his

anger toward Helene. "You didn't tell me you had a boyfriend."

Helene's mouth opened and closed without a sound coming out as if she were in shock.

Andrew released the doctor's shoulder, hoping he didn't wet the seat. "Well, now you know."

"I most certainly do," the doctor said. He edged away from Andrew. He looked like he was about to say something, then changed his mind, and strode off. The haste in his steps removed all dignity from his retreat.

With an amused grin, Andrew plopped in the chair on the other side of Helene. "I told you he was a douche. You're welcome."

"Which part am I supposed to be thanking you for? The part where you lied about being my boyfriend? Or when you threatened my date?" Helene didn't get angry often, but she'd had all day to fume over the kiss the man before her had given her earlier that day. That kiss had not only dominated her thoughts all afternoon, but it had killed any excitement she'd had about going out with Gil.

He crossed his arms across his chest. "You were cringing every time he touched you."

"That's not true," she protested, hating that it was. "Okay, so it wasn't going well, but that doesn't mean I wanted your help or that big, stupid, smug smile you're beaming at me. You should be apologizing. You embarrassed me."

His smile dimmed. "It was for your own good. A date

like that wasn't going to get better. They never do. Guys are assholes."

Helene waved her hand at him. "You'd know that better than I would—being both yourself."

The corner of his mouth twitched as if he were about to smile again. "My intention was not to embarrass you. That guy was a creep."

Helene took a deep calming breath, a long gulp of water, then another deep breath. She'd never had a man jump to her protection because it had never been an issue. "I appreciate that you wanted to help me, but your delivery sucked. I can only imagine what Gil is going to tell everyone back at the clinic. My uncle thought my presence at the hospital would help, but it's more like I'm single-handedly fueling the gossip mill."

"Your uncle?"

"Are you going to pretend you don't know who I am?"

"I'm not really the pretend-anything type."

That much she was beginning to believe. "I'm Dr. Clarence Stiles's niece."

She could have sworn he muttered, "That figures," but she wasn't certain.

"What did you say?"

"How long have you worked for him?"

"Why does that matter?" If he was after her uncle, she wasn't going to give him any information.

"I'm not sure it does."

Helene threw her hands up in the air with exasperation. "I know why you're talking to me."

"You do?"

"And it won't get you anywhere."

"No?" The smile returned to his face.

"No. Go back and tell whoever you're working for that trying to dig up dirt on my uncle was a waste of time. He's a good man who has not only run a successful clinic for over thirty years, but he has also done a lot for this community. Ask around, you won't find a single person who doesn't love him."

"Really? Care to test that?"

There was a challenge in his eyes that was infuriating and sexy at the same time. "Sure."

Andrew waved a waitress over. Of course, it had to the be the one that only a few minutes earlier she'd seen write her phone number on a napkin for him. The woman's expression turned guarded when Andrew asked her if she knew Clarence Stiles.

"Everyone knows him. He owns the largest private clinic on the island."

"How would you describe him?" Andrew pressed.

The woman shifted from one foot to another before answering. "He has done many good things for the people of Aruba."

"But?"

She looked around as if making sure she was not overheard. "Some people are too powerful to have an opinion about. They just are. I'm sorry, was that all? I have to get back to the kitchen."

"Yes, thank you," Andrew said slowly.

The exchange left Helene feeling uncomfortable and more than a little disloyal to her uncle. She took a few bills from her wallet and put them on the table. "Would you mind making sure the check gets paid? I have to go."

Andrew dropped another bill and joined her. "It'll be fine. I'll walk out with you."

She made it all the way outside the restaurant before she spun on him. "When I said I have to go, I meant without you."

He rubbed a hand over his face. "She didn't say anything bad about your uncle."

Helene waved a hand. "It wouldn't have mattered if she had. Tell her that when you sleep with her later."

He frowned. "When I what?"

Angry with herself for even caring, Helene glared at him. "I saw you take her number."

His hand went to the pocket where he'd placed the napkin. "And you thought we were hooking up?"

"I didn't think anything because I don't even know you. I couldn't care less about who you do what with."

The stupid grin returned to his face. "Liar. Don't worry, I didn't like the idea of creeper doctor touching you, either."

With a frustrated growl, Helene spun away and started walking. She hadn't brought a car because Gil had picked her up; she'd worry about how to get home later. Right then all she cared about was getting as far away from Andrew Smith as she could. She halted without looking back at him. "Is Andrew Smith even your name?"

"Andrew is."

I knew it. She forced herself to start walking again.

"Helene?" he called out softly.

She stopped again. "What?"

"You forgot something."

She instantly felt for her purse and was relieved she'd remembered to grab it. She opened it and did a quick check for her wallet and phone. By the time she looked up he was beside her. "I have everything," she said in confusion.

"Oh, then I forgot something." With that he cupped her face between his hands and kissed her with a boldness that shocked her into submission. His tongue teased her lips to open, and they did as if it were the most natural thing to do. As if kissing a complete stranger in the middle of a parking lot was something she did regularly. He explored her mouth with a gentleness she hadn't expected and with a thoroughness that had her melting against him.

A young female voice called out loudly, "Hypocrite."

Andrew broke off the kiss but continued to look into her eyes, his ragged breath warming her skin. "She's right. I am. But you do something to me."

Helene stepped back, covering her mouth with shaking fingers. He did something to her, too. He made her forget who he was and why it was important to stay away from him. "You need to stop kissing me."

"I'm trying," he said without humor. He studied her face. "Do you have a way to get home?"

"I'm not getting in a car with you."

"How about a cab I call for you?"

"Who are you?"

He seemed to consider his next words carefully before saying, "Andrew Barrington."

"Did someone send you to dig up dirt on my uncle?"

"No." She sagged with relief until he added, "They sent me to find a nurse who used to work for him."

"Why?"

Another long pause. "My brother died at your uncle's clinic twenty-nine years ago."

It took a moment to absorb what he was saying before asking, "How?"

"He was born prematurely."

"That's sad, but I don't understand why you'd think it was the clinic's fault."

"It probably wasn't. My brother asked me to find a nurse who worked there at that time. He thinks she might know something. I honestly can't imagine what he expects her to know, but I did promise to find her."

Helene thought back to the reason her uncle had asked her to work for him in the first place. "This might sound crazy, but someone was trying to bribe people in my department. Did you do that?"

"That wasn't me."

"Could it have been your family?"

He shrugged. Shrugged as if not knowing was acceptable. He'd already lied about who he was, would he lie about what he knew? She didn't want to think so, but she also couldn't believe him if that put her uncle in jeopardy.

My uncle would know how much of this is true. And maybe this is actually a better scenario than he thought it was. He thought someone was trying to take his clinic down, but instead it might just be a family who wants to know how their child died. Surely explaining something like that was an unfortunate side of working in health care, and her uncle would be comfortable with handling it.

"Would you come to dinner tomorrow night and meet my uncle? Perhaps your questions would be answered directly that way."

"Why would he tell me the truth?"

"Because he did nothing wrong. He has dedicated his life to helping people. When you meet him you'll see he isn't in this business for the money. He gives back more than he makes. If something did go wrong with your brother's birth, he would have done everything possible to save him."

He ran the back of his hand across her jaw and down the curve of her neck. "You sell him well."

"Because he's a good man," she said, feeling a little like someone who had gone too deep under the water and could no longer tell which way was up or down. *If I'm not supposed to be with this man, why does his touch feel so damn good?*

Andrew called a cab, and they waited in the parking lot, barely talking or looking at each other. Helene had waited twenty-six years to meet Mr. Right. She chewed her bottom lip and fought the realization that Mr. Right Here, Mr. Right Now . . . Mr. Take Me On the Hood of That Car . . . was *now* what she craved.

When the cab arrived she ducked into it quickly without giving him a chance to kiss her again or say anything else. If his lips found hers again, she feared she'd drag him into the cab and let everything else figure itself out after she discovered if what she'd been putting off was as good as everyone said it was.

He paid the driver while she was settling in. She rushed to tell him she didn't want his money, but it was too late.

He knocked on the window of the cab and handed her his phone number on a corner of the napkin the waitress had written her number on. If that wasn't a reminder that she needed to get control of herself, she didn't know what was.

"Call me with details about tomorrow," he said, his eyes holding hers intently.

"I will," she promised and rolled up the window before she said anything that would reveal how much she wanted to see him again.

Chapter Four

THE NEXT MORNING Andrew made meeting the private investigator part of his morning run. When he'd contacted the man via text he'd been told to go to the rocky side of the island and look for a man with black hair and a short beard just after the lighthouse. No one fitting that description was in the area and as Andrew dropped down to a walk, his senses went into high alert. Although there wasn't a person in sight, he knew he wasn't alone.

A decade of learning how to scout ahead without being seen had left him acutely aware of when there were eyes on him. No weapon. No armor. All he could do was wait for a movement and drop to the sand if he needed to. Beyond that, he would wait. There was no reason to think he was in danger—yet.

A tall blonde walked out from behind the lighthouse. In a sarong and sandals, she approached him, a colorful beach bag at her side. She looked like just another tourist in search of a sandy spot to sunbathe. The confident way she approached kept Andrew on alert. He couldn't pin down what made him not trust her, but he remained ready to hit the sand or her if he had to.

She stopped a couple feet away. "Stand down, Marine. I'm one of the good guys."

He didn't like how amused she was, like she was in a private joke he hadn't been told. "Do you work for the Shane Agency?"

She laid a towel out on the sand and sat down on it. "You're so cute. Sit down."

"No thanks," he said gruffly. "So, who are you?"

"A friend. A frustrated one, to be honest. Your family is not easy to help."

"I don't understand."

"If I do this myself, I'll be blamed for the fallout." She took out a paperback book and laid it open on her lap as if she'd been interrupted while reading. "People say they want the truth, but they don't. Take what happened in Iraq. I completely understand why you went along with the cover-up. The truth would devastate the families."

Fury surged through Andrew. He stepped forward, spraying sand across her legs as he did. "I don't know what the fuck you're talking about." Had Ahearn sent her? Was he being tested?

Calm and cool, she brushed the sand off. "It wasn't your fault. You couldn't have known. You don't believe that, but it's true."

Andrew turned and started to walk away from her. If she was there to see if he would confirm or deny the details, the best response was to disengage.

"So sensitive. Who knew? Unfortunately, we're not done

yet. I'm not here about why you left the Marines. I'm here about Helene Franklin."

That's it. Andrew spun back and advanced on her, not stopping until he was towering above her. "I'm listening, but I'd better like what you say."

The woman lifted her glasses just enough to study his face. "You sound like Asher when you're angry. It's a shame you're not closer, the two of you have a lot in common."

If she'd been a man, he'd have his hands around his throat, but instead he refocused on what she'd said that he actually cared about. "What about Helene?"

The woman rose to her feet, brushed herself off, and re-packed her bag. After slinging it over her shoulder, she said, "If you're not careful, you *will* get her killed." Andrew made a grab for the woman's arm, but she evaded him and added quickly, "Easy, tiger, I'm not the one who would hurt her. I'm on your side." She took out a black business card with a white phone number on one side and tossed it into the sand at his feet. As he rose from picking it up, he heard the hum of a helicopter, nothing unusual wherever there were tourists paying for tours, but this one was swooping down. She'd dashed just far enough away that when a rope fell she was able to grab it and be pulled out of his reach even though he ran to her.

As she rose, she yelled out, "Get a gun, Andrew. You'll need it. And don't trust anything her uncle says. Be the Barrington who actually impresses me." She waved before being hoisted up into the helicopter like some acrobat act.

Until then, Andrew would have said not much surprised

him anymore. However, he stood there, watching her helicopter disappear over the water and struggled to wrap his head around what had just happened. The whole exchange felt like a staged scene in a movie, a prank by one of his brothers. Except none of his brothers had much of a sense of humor, and she'd known things she couldn't.

Or did she?

She hadn't given particulars. It could be that she wanted him to think she knew more than she did.

Why?

And what did she mean about getting Helene killed?

"Andrew Barrington?" a man asked from behind him.

Andrew spun and delivered a powerful kick to the man's chest that sent him flying backward and landing in the sand. Andrew was on him, lifting him partially up by the collar of his shirt while shaking him. "Who's asking?"

"Creston Bray, from the Shane Agency. We have an appointment today," the man sputtered.

Black hair. Black beard. Andrew released him back into the sand. "Did you see the woman who was here a moment ago?"

Creston shook his head and slowly, shakily, rose to his feet. "I didn't see anyone. This beach is always deserted at this time of day which is why I chose it."

"Who did you tell that you were meeting me here?"

"No one."

Andrew flashed the black card in front of Creston's face. "What can you tell me about this?"

The man's eyes darted from the black business card to

Andrew's face and back. He wiped sweat from his brow. "Does it have a name on it?"

With a growl of frustration, Andrew pocketed the card. "Is there anything you do fucking know?"

HELENE HAD RISEN before the sun and been asking herself since then if suggesting Andrew meet her uncle had been wise. On the elevator ride up to her uncle's office at the clinic, she wondered again if there was a chance that Andrew, if *that* was his real name, had been manipulating her with meeting her uncle as his end goal the whole time.

By no stretch of the imagination could Andrew be described as stable. In between acting like he was attracted to her and couldn't stay away from her, she'd sensed moments when he seemed dangerously angry and on the verge of real violence. *That should not turn me on as much as it does.*

Why couldn't he be ugly? Why does this have to be so complicated?

Dangerous men aren't even my taste.

Do I even have a taste?

Oh, my God, I do and it's for really, really messed-up men.

Shit.

She greeted her uncle's secretary, Marcy, and asked if he was available.

"Always for you, sweetie. I'll tell him you're here."

The door opened and her uncle waved her in. "Good. I was hoping you'd come see me. I heard about something that we need to discuss."

Double shit. Does he know about Andrew? Is he upset that I waited until now to tell him?

Her uncle closed the door and pointed toward two chairs off to one side of his office. "Have a seat."

Helene did so and folded her hands on her lap. *I've done nothing wrong. I'll just tell him what I know.* "Uncle Clarence, I'm so sorry I didn't tell you last night, but it was late when I got back . . ."

He took the seat across from her. "I don't blame you for not saying anything. You were put in an awkward position."

"Yes," she said with a vehement nod. "Nothing like this ever happened to me before."

"Of course it didn't. Don't worry. I handled it. He won't bother you again."

A tightness spread across her chest. *Oh, no.* She felt sick. "What did you do?" her words came out as a whisper.

"I fired him. You're my niece. It was bad enough that he asked you out, but to dare to say anything derogatory about you here, to my staff, that was inexcusable."

Fired him? "Oh, you mean Dr. Gunder." Relief flooded through her, and she felt like a complete idiot for believing for a second that her uncle was capable of anything sinister.

"Yes, Dr. Gunder. Why, is someone else harassing you? Don't be afraid to give me their names. I have zero tolerance for that kind of thing. We're here to save lives not replicate scenes from daytime soap operas."

"No, everyone else has been wonderful."

Her uncle leaned forward and gave her knee a pat. "Since you said yes to Gunder, I know you must have been excited to have been asked out. Your mother explained to me that you've always had trouble finding dates. Don't worry. I know a lot of people. We'll find you someone nice."

Helene wished she could sink into the floor and disappear. "Please, don't listen to my mother. I'm fine."

"Of course." Her uncle sat back with a sympathetic smile. "We won't speak of this again, but I wanted you to know I take my role as your guardian seriously."

Guardian? "Uncle Clarence, I'm twenty-six, I don't need—"

"I may not have been around much while you were growing up, but having you here has reminded me of the importance of family. Whatever you need, Helene, all you have to do is ask. You said you wanted to go back to school. I want to help you make that happen."

Blinking back tears, Helene said, "I don't know what to say except thank you and I'm sorry I was the reason you had to let one of your doctors go. I should have known better than to agree to that date in the first place."

With a touch of sadness in his eyes, he said, "You've lived a sheltered life, Helene. Don't rush to shed that innocence. Trust me, it's not easy once it's gone."

Helene nodded because the truth of how much she wanted to ditch that innocence wasn't something she could share with her uncle. "I love you, Uncle Clarence."

His smile returned. "I love you, too, Lenny."

Helene's eyebrows shot up. "Don't you dare. It's bad enough my parents call me that."

He laughed heartily. "We used to call your mother Rosie Posie. Start throwing that back at her and your nickname will die away pretty quickly."

Smiling, Helene said, "Really? That's awesome. What else don't I know about her?"

Her uncle went on to share several more stories about what it had been like for them as children. His intent was to make Helene feel better, and it worked. She was smiling and laughing in no time.

Eventually her uncle glanced at the clock on the wall, stood, and said, "I hate to say it, but I have to get back to work. Was there anything else you needed?"

Helene smacked her forehead. *How could I forget?* "Yes. I met someone yesterday who asked me a question that I thought you'd be the better one to answer."

"Who did you meet?" he asked, already beginning to shuffle through papers.

Helene went to stand in front of his desk. "Andrew Barrington."

Her uncle went pale and sat down. "Where did you meet him?"

"Here at the clinic." She leaned forward. "Are you okay?"

Looking like he was far from fine, her uncle said, "Sorry, I got lightheaded for a moment. Probably because I skipped breakfast. Luckily I'm surrounded by doctors, right?"

"Do you want me to call someone?" she asked in a mild panic.

"No. No. They nag me enough about my blood sugar. I'll have Marcy bring me a snack after you go." He rested his hands on his desk. "Now, tell me about this Andrew Barrington. What did he want to know?"

"We don't have to talk about this now. It's nothing." The last thing she wanted to do was add to her uncle's stress, especially when he wasn't feeling well.

"Tell me," her uncle said in a harsh tone she'd never heard him use. Her shock must have shone on her face because he grimaced. "Sorry, I get testy when my BSL is low." He picked up his phone and asked his secretary to have orange juice sent up from the cafeteria. "Now, what were you saying?"

"Just that the question can wait."

"What was it? His question. What did he ask you?"

"It's about his brother. He died at birth in this clinic twenty-nine years ago. The family is still wondering how it happened. I told Andrew if he had a question about it he should ask you directly." Her next suggestion sounded ridiculous as she said it now. "I thought we could have him over tonight for dinner. It's Andrew's family who are pushing for answers. He understands that awful things like that can happen no matter how good the care is. I thought if you met with him it might smooth the whole thing over."

"Why are they asking about this now?"

"He didn't say."

Her uncle brought a shaking hand up to smooth his hair back. "Did he say anything else? Ask about anyone else?"

"Not really. I mean, yes. A nurse. He said his family asked him to find the nurse who had worked for you during that time."

"What was her name?"

"Pamela Thorsen."

"That's it? That's all he said?"

"Yes."

"Are you sure?"

"Absolutely." Helene didn't want to ask, but she had to. "Do you remember his family? I know it was a long time ago."

Her uncle's face tightened. "You never forget the ones you lose. I remember the Barringtons. They're an extremely wealthy family from Boston."

Wealthy? Andrew didn't give off that vibe at all. "And the baby that died?"

Her uncle stood and walked to the window of his office. "Nothing could be done to prevent what happened." He turned back to face her. "Did you say you invited Andrew Barrington to dinner?"

"I told him I'd ask you."

"Do it. Invite him for seven. We'll have a late meal."

Helene hesitated. "Are you sure you're up to it?"

His smile looked forced. "I'll be fine."

Unsure of what to say or do next, Helene just stood there feeling like she'd let him down.

As he often did, he seemed to read her mind. "You did the right thing, Helene. If his family has concerns, it's our duty to help them find some peace." He referenced the clock again. "Now, if you don't mind, I have too much to do and not enough hours in the day to get it done."

"Of course," Helene said. She started walking to the door, stopped, and rushed over to her uncle to give him a hug. "Thank you for being so good to me."

He kissed her forehead. "If I had a daughter, I'd like to think she would have turned out like you. The world looks better when I see it through your eyes." He turned away again. "Now go on. Get back to work."

"See you tonight," she said just before she closed the door.

He didn't answer, but she didn't wait for him to. Her uncle was a busy man. He had, though, agreed to meet Andrew and, hopefully, that would bring a good conclusion to a very confusing couple of days.

I'll see Andrew tonight.

Most likely, for the last time.

He'll have his answers and there'll be no reason for us to see each other again.

Chapter Five

STILES'S HOUSE WASN'T the mammoth structure Andrew had expected. It wasn't small, nor was it flashy. It was a villa on a hill, stucco exterior, muted colors, a gated home within a gated community, on a third of an acre with nothing blocking the view from the street. A guesthouse flanked one side with not so much as a tree blocking it from the main home. Stiles seemed to value security over aesthetics, which was a curious position for a supposedly beloved benefactor.

Andrew pressed the video intercom on the stone pillar at the gate and announced his arrival. A man responded, telling him to pull up and park in front of the far left garage, and Andrew did so after the gate swung open. Before getting out, he leaned over, opened the glove compartment of his car, and tucked a 9mm Berretta in the back of his trousers. He didn't think there would be a need for it, but he hadn't taken the advice he'd gotten on the beach that morning lightly. When someone yells duck, a wise man does so first and figures out the nature of the threat later.

"If you're not careful, you will get her killed," the anonymous blonde had said. Careful about what? She hadn't exactly been specific with her warnings. Was his association with Helene putting her in danger because of who he was, because of something her uncle had done, or for some completely unrelated issue someone was afraid he'd stumble upon? The blonde had known about Iraq, or implied she had. Was the threat against *him* because of what he knew, and Helene was someone Ahearn might use against him? None of it made sense. He'd tried to call the number on the card, but it had rung many times without answer. Not exactly the helpline the blonde had implied it would be.

As Andrew walked up the many steps of the villa, he asked himself if it was wise to be there at all. The last thing he wanted was the blood of another person on his hands. And for what?

My brother sent me to find out about a death that happened nearly thirty years ago. Even if the clinic was at fault, what would the truth change? Nothing. If negligence was a pattern of behavior, Dr. Clarence Stiles wouldn't still be in business.

Does any of this matter enough to put an innocent woman's life at risk?

If she is innocent.

She definitely had nothing to do with what had happened twenty-nine years ago, but there was no way to know what her uncle might be mixed up in now.

I could leave now. Andrew hesitated before ringing the doorbell. *However, if my presence here is a danger to Helene, how safe is she anyway? I can't walk away before I know who would hurt her and why.*

Recon without engagement is no longer an option, but I'm not going in blind. If there is a lurking threat, I will find and neutralize it. Helene Franklin is not dying on my watch.

He squared his shoulders and rang the doorbell.

The door flew open, revealing the woman he couldn't shake from his thoughts. She wore a navy blue dress that was modest and sexy at the same time. The excitement in her eyes accompanied by the pink flush on her cheeks made him want to pull her to him and kiss her soundly. The presence of the suited man at her side, though, kept Andrew in check. He looked the man over from head to foot and frowned. This wasn't her uncle. This man was heavier, older, and had the polite air of someone who was paid to be welcoming.

"I have it, Paul," Helene said in a rush.

"As you wish," the man said before retreating into the home.

Helene smiled at Andrew, and he felt a surprising warmth. "You look beautiful," he said.

"Thank you." Her smile widened. "I never know what to wear to dinner here. My uncle is on the formal side. I grew up on a large animal rescue and rehab facility. Back there, we wiped our feet, washed our hands, and that was good enough."

The more he learned about her, the more she fascinated him. She took sweet to a level that bordered on unbelievable. In his experience, people pretended to be good, but if you scratched their surface you discovered an entirely different side of them. An animal rescue? Seriously? She was hard selling not only her uncle's good nature, but a positive image of herself as well. No one was that good. Instead of sharing any of those thoughts, he chose to keep their conversation light. "You washed your hands? That's considered a luxury in some of the places I've spent time."

She opened the door wider. "Come in." She bit her lip and looked uncertain. "My uncle isn't here yet. He said to start without him because he'd be late. I should have called you when I found out. I hope you don't consider this a waste of your ti—"

Her huge-eyed innocence act was too much. He had to know how much he knew about her was an act and how much was real. There was one surefire way to find out. He held the door with one hand and backed her up against it with one strong move, digging his other hand into the back of her hair to hold her head still for his plundering kiss. Her arms slid up to loop around his neck, and she arched against him. He was rock hard and loving every place her body touched his. Her mouth opened for him, and he lost himself in the sweet taste of her.

The reason he'd initiated their kiss fell to the wayside as fireworks shot through him, overwhelming him. He'd been numb for so long that feeling anything, even something this good, was painful. Desire for her cut through his guilt, his shame, and made a mockery of his willpower. Sinner or saint, he didn't care which she was. Whatever she wanted, he wanted to give her as she kept rubbing herself back and forth against his cock.

Her hands slid down his chest, across his stomach, and he thought he might come from the unexpected pleasure of them gripping his ass. She was bold in her exploration. It was difficult to believe she was a virgin, but, holy shit. Now, he wanted her to be. He wanted to be the first one to taste her, the only one. His completely primitive and possessive desire to own her fueled his need for her. Lost in the heat of their passion, he could have taken her right there in the hallway of her uncle's home. She kissed him with total abandon that said she wanted the same.

Her hands moved upward over his belt. He knew the exact moment she grazed the gun because she tensed and broke off the kiss.

Between ragged breaths, she asked, "Is that a—do you have a—?"

Where he was, pressed up against her, he felt her heart beating wildly in her chest. It wasn't only passion he saw in her eyes; there was also fear. "Yes."

She kept her eyes focused on his neck and dropped her arms away. "Why would you bring one here?"

He gripped her chin with more force than he meant to and brought her face upward until her eyes met his. "You said you weren't afraid of me."

"I'm trying not to be."

Her honesty brought a small smile to his lips. "But your instincts tell you I'm dangerous?"

She looked away then back. "Sometimes," she whispered.

He released her chin and brought his hand down her neck, marveling at the delicacy of it as he caressed it. "Do you know who everyone says are the most deadly people to deal with?"

"No." She swallowed visibly, looking both turned on and more than a little afraid of him. He didn't mind either reaction.

She needed to be careful when it came to him. He was damaged, and if she was half as innocent as she portrayed herself to be, the right thing to do would be to help her without giving in to the temptation of her. His need for her was battling with what was left of his moral code, and it was winning. He continued, "A man who has nothing left to lose or one willing to give his life to protect someone. I am both."

Her eyes widened. "I don't understand. Who do you feel you need to protect?"

"You." His answer hung in the air for a long moment.

Chapter Six

>>>>>><<<<<<

M *E?*

Maybe it was the sensation of being so physically close to him or the strength he exuded—*and good Lord can the man kiss*—but she believed him. She didn't think she was in danger, but she believed he *thought* she was. Was this what was referred to as Post Traumatic Stress Disorder? She didn't know. She had no experience with it, at least not in humans, but she knew how animals dealt with stress. Some withdrew. Some lashed out. Often the brutalized ones saw an enemy in every extended hand. They were the most dangerous ones.

And he has a gun.

"Who do you think I need protecting from?" she asked and held her breath as she awaited his answer.

"I'm not sure." There was the slightest falter in his confidence, one she would have missed if she hadn't been watching his reaction closely.

She let out a slow breath and spoke in the tone she used at the rescue whenever she approached a volatile resident. "You don't have to protect me, Andrew. I'm not in any danger."

His only answer was a clenching and releasing of a hand at his side.

In a calm tone, she suggested, "Why don't you give me the gun?"

He ran his hands down her arms in a final caress then stepped back. "What time is your uncle expected?"

A chill passed through her, and she considered calling the authorities. *But what would I say? He hasn't threatened my uncle or me. He's here because we invited him.* "He didn't say, but I think you should leave."

He frowned and studied her face. "I would never hurt you."

She kept her shoulders squared and held his eyes. "I don't want you to hurt *anyone*. Please leave."

He rubbed a hand roughly over his chin. "I know you have no reason to trust me, but I can't leave until I know you're safe."

"You said you were here to find out about your brother. Was that another lie?"

"No. That's what brought me to Aruba, but my presence here has put you at risk. I just don't know how yet."

She nodded slowly as her mind raced. The man before her was waging a battle with himself. "Andrew, something happened to you, didn't it? Something traumatic. How you're feeling is normal, but what you don't want to do is act on fears that aren't based in reality and yours aren't."

"I'm not afraid," he said in a cold tone.

No. He clearly wasn't. "Neither am I." It was a standoff of sorts. They simply stood there, painfully sexually aware of each other, breathing deeply, while also completely at odds. "We had a bull elephant come to our rescue once. He'd mauled the owner of an amateur traveling circus who had purchased him. He was angry, and even my parents wondered if he could be saved. He never charged at me because he knew I wasn't afraid of him. I respected what he'd been through. I knew all he wanted was to find his herd again. I believe you don't want to hurt me, but I do think you're dangerous, and you will be until you talk to someone about whatever happened to you."

He tensed and snapped. "You think you understand me? You don't."

"I'm not your enemy, Andrew."

He relaxed visibly and rubbed a hand over his face as if wiping away a memory. "What happened to that elephant?"

The memory of its fate brought tears to her eyes. "We placed him with an animal sanctuary in South Africa, but he didn't adapt. He became a danger to himself and those around him, and eventually they put him down. I don't know what you're doing in Aruba, or what you're doing with me, but I won't let you hurt my uncle." She motioned toward the still open door. "You should go."

FOR SEVERAL LONG moments, Andrew stood motionless. He was a man of action, not reflection or indecision. Stay or go. The choice was simple. Or was it? He kept circling back to what the woman on the beach had said that morning. *If I'm not careful, I'll get Helene killed.*

Right now, I'm as far from careful as I've ever been.

Dammit.

He straightened and stepped toward the door. The temptation to calm the chaos within him with alcohol was strong, but he wouldn't go down that road again. He marveled for a moment at how, even though she knew next to nothing about him, she understood him with uncomfortable clarity. *I'm a fucking angry elephant.* He breathed out a self-deprecating laugh.

She searched his face, and there was a realness to the moment that had him admitting, "I used to always know the right thing to do. I believed in my country, the Corps, and myself . . . often in that order. I don't know what I believe anymore."

She pressed her lips together with cautious sympathy. "I'm sorry for whatever happened to you."

"Because of me," he said harshly.

She nodded, seeming to understand how that was worse. He took another step through the door.

"Good," a male voice said as he came up the steps. "I don't appear to be too late."

The man stopped in front of Andrew and held out his hand in greeting. He was a dignified man in his sixties, slight of build but with a presence of someone important. "Although I hear the reason for your visit is not a happy one, it's a pleasure to meet you, Mr. Barrington. I'm Clarence Stiles." The man presented well. He looked Andrew in the eye and shook his hand firmly.

"Andrew was just saying that he can't stay," Helene said in a rush.

"Was he?" Clarence looked to Andrew in question.

Leaving was probably for the best until he knew more about the situation. Andrew needed time to clear his head. "My intention was not to intrude, and Helene mentioned that you unexpectedly had to work late. I'll come back another time."

Her uncle waved that idea away. "Nonsense. We're all here, and I'm sure my cook has prepared something delicious for tonight. Close the door, Helene, before you let bugs in."

Andrew met Helene's eyes again. "It's better if I go."

Stiles looked from Andrew to Helene. "Is there anything you'd like to tell me?" When Helene didn't immediately answer, he continued, "It appears that Dr. Gunder had a distinct lack of discretion. I heard a rumor this afternoon, Helene, that you have a possibly criminal, muscular giant of a new boyfriend. I'm assuming he was referring to you, Mr. Barrington."

Andrew cocked an eyebrow at the line of logic her uncle was drawing. He wasn't, however, about confirm or deny the rumor.

"We—I—" Helene stumbled to a stop, regrouped, then started again. "Andrew saw my date going badly and intervened. He said he was my boyfriend simply so Dr. Gunder would leave."

Stiles's eyes flew back to meet Andrew's sharply. "So you lied to and intimidated the doctor?"

Andrew shrugged. "I didn't like the way he was treating your niece."

Stiles clapped a hand on Andrew's shoulder and a smile

stretched his lips. "Good." He nodded and guided Andrew back inside the door. "I respect a man who isn't afraid to do the right thing. It's often not easy."

"No, sir."

Stiles closed the door. "How about a Scotch? You earned a drink."

Although Andrew allowed himself to be brought back into the home, he said, "I appreciate the offer, but I don't drink." Helene searched his face with such earnest intensity he found himself adding, "Anymore." He hated how pale she was. Her hands were clasped in front of her, and she looked on the verge of telling her uncle that he was a gun-carrying wack job. "I really can't stay." He took a step back.

Stiles looked at both of them again. "As you wish, but I was hoping I would have a chance to answer your questions. Helene told me your family still has concerns, and I'd like to put them to ease." The hand he ran through his hair shook.

Helene was at his side instantly. "Are you still feeling off? What was your blood sugar level when you last checked?"

"Enough, Helene. I'm fine. Maybe a little stressed." He looked over at Andrew. "We haven't lost many patients here. The memory of your brother's death weighs heavily on me even after all this time. I'd rather discuss it now instead of later unless there is a reason Mr. Barrington can't stay for dinner."

Helene shot Andrew a pleading look. It seemed to say, *Help him. Help us.* What he struggled with was if that was best done by staying or leaving.

"Andrew. Call me Andrew, and I could stay for a quick

meal. I appreciate you taking the time to address questions about something that happened so long ago."

"Perfect," Stiles said. "Then if you don't mind I'll take a moment to freshen up and meet both of you in the dining room. Helene, be a dear and make sure he has everything he needs."

"Of course, Uncle Clarence." She smiled until the exact moment her uncle disappeared into a room off the main foyer then her expression went stone cold. She spun and jabbed a finger into Andrew's chest. "My uncle isn't well. If you hurt him or upset him, I will . . . I will . . . I'll do something awful to you."

He'd never seen a more adorable sight than her snarling like a mama protecting her cub. He took her hand in his and brought it to his lips for a brief kiss. "I'll stay on my best behavior."

Desire battled with confusion in her eyes and she ripped her hand away from him. "I've seen your behavior, and I'm not sure your best is good enough."

A slow grin spread across his face, which gained him a glare from her. He couldn't help it, despite everything else, being with her felt good. She was quirky and upbeat, which would have normally annoyed him, but he remembered how she'd looked when she'd closed her eyes and held her face up to the warmth of the sun. That's how he felt near her. In a world that had become cold and empty to him, being near her felt so good he wanted to close his eyes and savor her.

Even if she looked as if she wanted to slap him.

"How are you a virgin?" He hadn't meant to utter the

question aloud, but he did softly, and she gasped when she heard him.

Between gritted teeth, she asked, "How are you not?"

He threw his head back and laughed at that. He'd been raised to tread lightly around women. The number-one rule in the Barrington home had always been to never ever upset their mother. Women were fragile. They could never be exposed to the harsher realities of life. Andrew had always avoided what some would consider *good* women. He didn't want to spend his life walking on eggshells, worried that one honest word from him would shatter his partner. Helene wasn't like that. When he pushed, she pushed back, and it excited him. He bent so he could whisper in her ear. "You are so damn hot."

She let out a shaky breath. "Right."

He raised his head and came to a sudden, shocking realization: Helene Franklin didn't know she was drop-dead gorgeous. It made him want to drag her out of there, forget about everything else, and show her exactly how beautiful she was . . . again and again, all night long. And he was sure every ounce of his desire was written on his face.

"Helene?" Stiles called from the dining room.

Oh, yes, dinner. He groaned. His only consolation was the look of yearning in her eyes that mirrored the need gnawing at him.

He didn't want to want her, but that horse had left the stable.

He didn't want to doubt her or her uncle, but that required disregarding what the woman on the beach had said.

Who may have been sent to test me rather than actually deliver that message. What she said about Helene could have been a veiled warning of what would happen if I didn't keep my mouth shut about what happened in Iraq. Although, if Colonel Ahearn were going to threaten me, I can't imagine it would have come in the form of a high-drama blonde. More likely it would have been a near miss from a .50 caliber sniper rifle. Close enough to get the point across without adding to the colonel's headcount. Or more accurately—deadcount.

No, it doesn't make sense for the colonel to send the blonde.

Someone is fucking with me, but I don't know who or why yet.

"Answer him," he commanded softly.

She searched his face again. "First, promise me you'll go easy on him."

He felt jaded and old before such an innocent request. If he actually were there to mess with her uncle, any promise made would have been an empty one. He didn't have to ask her, though, if she still believed that a man's word meant something—the answer was there in her eyes. Despite everything, she still trusted him to do the right thing because he fucking *promised* to. Someone would teach her that believing anyone inevitably led to disappointment, but he didn't want to be that person. "I will." And he would, unless her uncle gave some indication that he was a threat to her. After leaving the Corps, he didn't think he would ever again have the stomach to take someone out, but he pitied the person who tried to hurt Helene. Emmitt had said every Marine, even retired ones, needed a mission. Keeping Helene safe had become his last stand, not because he knew her very well, but because something told him that saving her was the key to saving himself, and if she died on his watch he was headed somewhere dark, a place there was no turning back from.

She touched his arm gently as if she could see the tortured corners of his mind. "Thank you." Then she called out, "Coming, Uncle Clarence."

They walked toward the dining room side by side. Before entering, she looked up at him and said, "After tonight it would probably be best if we don't see each other again."

He didn't answer her because that was one promise he wasn't willing to make.

A FEW MINUTES later, Helene thanked the woman who placed a plate of food in front of her. *I should ask my uncle for a moment alone. He needs to know Andrew has a gun. He needs to know there is a pain bubbling within his guest that might be about more than his brother's death. He was too volatile for it to be about something that happened decades before. If she told her uncle, he might be able to get him help.*

She rested her chin on her hand as she listened to Andrew and her uncle make small talk. She'd expected him to eat like a starved animal or speak with his mouth full, but his dining etiquette was impeccable. *Because he was brought up by a wealthy family.* It was easy to forget that.

Why would a man who had everything leave that lifestyle behind to become a Marine? And what is it that brings such a desolation to his eyes that I can feel his sadness?

No. No. No. He's not a wounded animal in need of rescuing. Don't look at him that way. He's a man. A gorgeous, armed, potentially dangerous man.

Who makes me want to throw all sense to the wind and beg to be taken. Just any man won't be good enough anymore. I want my first time to be with someone who makes my body quiver with need just by looking at me. I want to know where this level of lust takes a person, could take me.

As Andrew reached for a piece of bread the muscles in his arm and shoulders flexed and bulged. Helene sighed. She reminded herself that he was a very troubled person, but her body betrayed her by continuing to lust over him.

Her gaze followed Andrew's strong hand as it closed around a glass of water. There was nothing sexy about him lifting it up to his mouth, parting those deliciously bold lips of his, and welcoming that cool water over his talented tongue, but it had her nearly drooling. The smile he shot her when he looked over and caught her watching him was just about the sexiest thing she'd ever seen.

Please don't let him be a psycho killer.

Andrew turned his attention back to her uncle. "So, you remember my parents."

"Yes," her uncle said. "Most of the local people use the maternity ward at the public hospital, but your father wanted the best for your mother so they came here. It was devastating for everyone involved when one of the babies didn't survive."

"Was there anything unusual about the delivery?" Andrew's tone was as casual as if he were asking about the weather the day before.

As he spoke to Andrew, her uncle moved his napkin from his lap to the table then back to his lap. The fidgeting was uncharacteristic and made Helene wonder whether her uncle was actually threatened by Andrew. *Why would he be, though?*

Her uncle said, "I don't remember there being anything, but it was a very long time ago. I tried to pull up records from that time, but it was before we updated our newest computer system and not all of the records, especially the older ones, were transferred over."

Andrew nodded. "I appreciate your patience with these questions. My brother has it in his head that something happened and was covered up."

Her uncle's fork clattered against his plate before he set it down beside it. "I can assure you—"

Helene leaned forward and began her own protest.

With a raised hand, Andrew said, "Don't worry, I didn't come here expecting to uncover any wrongdoing. When I go back I plan to suggest he throw the journal out."

"What journal?" her uncle asked in a strangled tone that made Helene wonder if she shouldn't call a doctor and ask Andrew to leave. Her uncle was pale and sweaty. He was obviously putting on a brave face because he wanted to help Andrew, but he needed to think about himself and his health.

She had to get Andrew out of there.

"Andrew, didn't you say you had somewhere you needed to be?" Helene asked while sending him a silent, but clear message with her eyes.

Chapter Seven

ANDREW'S INSTINCTS TOLD him to stay, but those same instincts had failed him recently with deadly consequences. If he wasn't aware that his decision, whether to leave or remain, might endanger Helene's life, he wouldn't second-guess himself. When he looked in her eyes he didn't see just her. She was Lofton's wife asking him how her husband had died. She was the mother of Melbourne asking if her son had suffered. Andrew wanted to do right by Helene, as he'd wanted to do by them, but what that looked like was just as complicated this time around.

Did I fail my men and their families so completely that I'm being tested again? This time by a higher power? If so, I have bad news for God, I still don't fucking know what You want me to do.

I do know what Helene wants, though. She wants me to leave so that's what I'll do. He nodded, placed him napkin beside his plate, and stood. "You're right. Thank you for a wonderful meal."

Stiles quickly rose to his feet. He was sweaty and shaky, but Helene had said he wasn't feeling well. He said, "You must stay for dessert. My cook makes the most wonderful pastries."

"I would, but regrettably this is a commitment I can't get out of." *A promise.*

Helene rushed around the table to stand beside him. "I'll walk you out." She looked her uncle over again and added, "Will you be okay?"

There was a flash of impatience in her uncle's expression then he smiled at Andrew. "My niece worries about me more than she should. I understand, though, that she does it because she loves me. I imagine your brother sent you here out of his love for your parents as well. Are you very close to your family?"

Andrew shook his head. "Not since I joined the Marines."

"And why did you? Join the Marines, I mean."

It was an unexpected question, and one that Andrew now found difficult to answer. "I saw people who were wrapped up in their comfortable homes and their gadgets, people who didn't realize that none of what they had would be possible if someone wasn't out there fighting the ones who wanted to take it from them. I thought I could make a difference."

"You wanted to be a hero," Stiles said in a strange tone.

"Doesn't everyone?" Andrew asked with a heavy layer of self-deprecation.

"Not everyone," Stiles said in an odd, sad tone.

He's not dangerous. And Helene isn't afraid of him. It's time for me to go. He looked down at Helene who looked con-

cerned for both of them now. Only because Andrew preferred to see fire rather than worry in her eyes, he asked,
"What do you want to be when you grow up, Helene?" The
glare she sent him brought a smile back to his lips.

She linked her arm with his and began to physically drag
him with her. "Such a shame you can't stay longer."

To Andrew's surprise, Stiles walked with them to the
door. He shook Andrew's hand and asked, "How long will
you be in Aruba?"

Andrew glanced down at Helene before answering. "I
haven't decided yet."

"If time allows, we would love to have you visit again,"
Stiles said.

"Thank you," Andrew answered. "You *will* see more of
me." Although he was speaking to Stiles, his words were
meant for Helene. She'd released his arm as they neared the
door, and he was already aching for her touch.

Her eyes widened. Those delicious lips of hers parted
again and more than anything, he wanted Stiles to leave so
he could kiss her one more time.

"Helene, please give me a moment alone with Andrew,"
Stiles said, and Andrew groaned inwardly. If Stiles was guilty
of anything, it was being oblivious to when his presence
wasn't necessary.

"Okay," Helene said slowly. "I'll meet you back in the
dining room."

Stiles nodded and opened the front door. He closed it
once he and Andrew were through it. He walked over to
look down the street from the balcony. "It's obvious that

you've taken an interest in my niece."

Oh, shit. He's not as oblivious as I thought. "She's a beautiful woman."

Leaning forward on the railing of the balcony, Stiles said, "She is. Not just on the surface, but right through to her core. You don't meet many people like that. People usually have something they're hiding, a demon they'd do anything to escape but can't. Do you know what I'm saying?"

"I think so," Andrew said although he wasn't sure he did.

"Either you know or you don't. We're all defined by our worst day, aren't we? It doesn't matter how much good we do before or after, we never rise above our lowest moment."

"Say whatever it is you're dancing around," Andrew ordered between clenched teeth. *If this is a threat to expose me because he somehow knows about what happened in Iraq, bring the threat on. I'm not the one desperate to keep the truth hidden.*

Stiles turned and met his eyes. "I need you to take Helene back to her parents. I should have never let her come here."

Andrew stepped closer and growled. "Take her back? Why? Is she in danger?"

Stiles paled. "I love my niece. She shouldn't be involved in any of this. I would send her away myself, but I don't know who I can trust. It may already be too late for all of us."

Grabbing Stiles's arm, Andrew gave him a shake. "What are you talking about?"

"Whose journal were you referring to earlier?"

Eyes narrowed, Andrew said, "Patrice Stanfield's."

"How did you get it?"

Andrew shrugged impatiently. "It came to our family when she died."

Stiles's arm shook beneath his hold. "How did she die?"

"Heart failure?" Andrew wasn't sure. He'd heard about her passing, but since he'd never had a relationship with her he hadn't paid much attention to the details. "What does any of this have to do with Helene being in danger?"

Stiles tried to pull away, but Andrew held him easily. "Get a private plane. Leave Aruba and take Helene with you. Right now. Don't take your eyes off her for a moment until she's back in Florida. If you care for her at all, do this. And don't tell her anything. The more she knows the more danger she'll be in."

Tightening his hand on the older man's arm, Andrew said, "I'm not doing anything until you explain what this is all about."

The man's eyes filled with tears. "Nothing I could say would change the past. It wouldn't bring your brother back."

My brother? How is this about him? How could what happened back then be dangerous now? "What the hell are you talking about? What are you not telling me?"

"Your brother's death wasn't an accident."

And whoosh, just like that, Andrew was in fighter mode. He gripped both of the man's arms and lifted him off his feet, shaking him violently. "What do you mean it wasn't an accident?"

Stiles slumped in Andrew's hold. "I'm so sorry. God, it feels good to finally say it. It's my fault you lost your brother.

I hate the choices I made, and that I kept the truth to myself. If this were just about me, I would tell you everything, but I don't matter anymore. She does. You need to get her out of here." The agony in Stiles's eyes mirrored Andrew's own torment, and he began to lower Stiles to his feet.

"PUT HIM DOWN," Helene screamed from the doorway as soon as the initial shock of the scene before her passed. Even though she'd only frozen for a second, it had felt longer as she watched the man she'd brought into her uncle's home maul him like some kind of wild animal. Without hesitation she attacked, pulling at the closest arm to her that was holding her uncle while kicking at his legs. "Let go of him." Andrew released her uncle, but Helene kept kicking and hitting him. "I trusted you and this is what you do?"

Andrew fended her off easily simply by placing a hand on her shoulder and keeping her slightly off balance. She tried to push his hand away but all those muscles she'd found attractive earlier were now her enemies. She yanked herself free from his hold and went to stand protectively in front of her uncle while frantically digging through her bra for the phone she'd stashed there. Her hands were shaking as she swiped the phone. "I'm done. I'm calling the police. Don't come back here, Andrew. Ever. If you do, I'll make sure they arrest you. I'm sorry, but you're not stable. You need help."

Her uncle took the phone out of her hands. "You can't make that call, Helene."

"Yes, I can. We have to, Uncle Clarence. He's more dangerous than you know." *Please hold it together long enough for me to get you help.*

Her uncle put a hand on her arm and said, "Calm down, Helene. You need to calm down."

Shaking her head, Helene looked back and forth between her uncle and Andrew. *I have to say it, even if it incites Andrew.* "He has a gun."

"Good," her uncle said.

Helene's mouth dropped open as she tried to wrap her head around her uncle's reaction. "Good? Good? He could kill us both. We need to call the police."

Her uncle stepped forward and took her hand in his. "I love you, Helene. Do you believe that?"

"Yes," Helene said, feeling bile rise in her throat. Was he about to do something heroic like attack Andrew himself? Andrew would kill him.

"Then go with Andrew. Don't ask me why. Don't take time to pack. Get in his car and go. Now."

"No," Helene said, frantically trying to figure out how any of this made sense. She met Andrew's eyes and said firmly, "I'm not going anywhere with him."

"Yes, you are," her uncle said, looking fragile and scared.

She shook her head vehemently. "Absolutely not."

Her uncle opened the door and called for Paul to retrieve her purse and passport. A few minutes later, he dismissed Paul then handed Helene's phone, passport, and purse to Andrew. "Get her out of here."

Tears filled Helene's eyes as she continued to scramble to understand what was going on. "Why do you want me to go with him? Why aren't you trying to protect me *from* him?"

Shaking and with tears in his own eyes, her uncle said, "I'm so sorry, Helene. I wish I could explain it to you. You have to trust me, or you'll get us both killed. This is the only way."

Helene gripped her uncle's forearm. "No, it's not. This is insane. I don't understand what's going on, but I can guarantee you I'm not getting in a car with him."

Her uncle shook her hand off, and when he spoke his tone sent a chill down Helene's spine. "If you love me at all, go with him, Helene. I know you don't understand, but it's better if you don't. If there were any other way, I wouldn't do this, but I have no choice. You have no choice. Andrew, she's all yours now."

With that, her uncle spun on his heel and retreated through the door, closing it behind him. Shocked into momentary silence, Helene simply stared at Andrew.

He reached for her arm. "We need to go, Helene."

She recoiled from him. "Don't touch me. You're a sick bastard. What did you have to threaten my uncle with to get him to do this?"

He stepped closer, with her purse still in one hand. "I didn't threaten him."

She retreated another step, looking around for an escape route. "Is this some kind of white slavery thing because I'm a virgin? If so, you need to know that technically I'm not. I touched Gerald Finley's penis my junior year, and I'm pretty sure he had an orgasm in his pants from it."

One of Andrew's eyebrows arched and he lunged for her, grabbing one of her arms with the speed and precision of a striking snake. "You're still a virgin, but you're safe. No one is going to hurt you. You haven't been sold. In fact, I'm going to help you."

She struggled to free herself but couldn't. "No, you're not."

He started to walk. She dug in her heels, but he pulled her behind him as if she were a reluctant child being dragged off by a parent. "Trust me, this wasn't my plan."

She tried to grab the banister on the way down, but wasn't strong enough to hold on. "I'll scream and I'll keep screaming until someone else calls the police."

Andrew paused at that. "You heard your uncle. Are you willing to risk your life as well as his?"

"Is that what you threatened him with? That you'd kill him and me? Maybe that worked on him, but I'm not an old man. You're not scaring me. I'll kill you right back."

He looked down at her. "That doesn't even make sense."

She growled in frustration as he unlocked the passenger side of his car. "You really think you can get me in that car?"

"Do you value your uncle's life?"

Helene glanced back at her uncle's door, which was still closed. *Why would he do this to me? Is he only playing along to give the police time to arrive? He could be on the phone with them now. That's it. He must have known Andrew has a gun, and he said what he had to, to buy himself time so he could save me.* No other possibility made sense. "Yes, I do."

"Then get in the car," Andrew ordered.

If I fight him here, maybe he'll go back in and kill my uncle before the police have a chance to arrive. No. He can't be a killer.

Why, because gorgeous people can't be evil? Really, what else does he need to do to prove to me that he's not sane?

He opened the car door, and she allowed herself to be pushed inside. It wasn't as if they were in the woods. They would still have to stop at several red lights, and when they did she would jump out.

He walked around to the driver's side, tossed her purse in the backseat, and slid in. He started the engine and said, "There's no reason to be afraid, Helene. I would never hurt you." She gasped at the brush of his arm across her breast as he reached to buckle her in. "I only want you to be safe."

"Then let me go back to my uncle."

Before answering, he reversed down the driveway, through the gate that automatically opened for them, and pulled out onto the street. "I wish I could, but I can't."

She studied his profile, looking for any hint as to what he was thinking. "Maybe you're confused or maybe you're angry at my uncle, but you don't have to do this. You haven't hurt anyone yet. Not really. Stop and let me out. I won't call the police. I promise."

He removed a hand from the steering wheel to rub his forehead as if he had a headache. "I am confused and angry, but that's not why I'm doing this."

She would have asked him why, but he looked distracted enough that she jumped at the opportunity to escape. She grabbed the wheel and pulled it in her direction, causing the car to nearly hit a pole. He swore, righted the car, then pulled over. "What are you trying to do, get us both fucking killed?" he yelled.

"Yes," she yelled back and released the seat belt. She turned her back to the car door and kicked him in the jaw. The move stunned him, and she was able to open her door and scramble to her feet on the sidewalk before he had a chance to stop her. There were people out, but they were far away, too far to hear her unless she screamed. She opened her mouth to do just that, but he grabbed her, spun her, and placed his hand over her mouth.

"I'm trying to help you," he said angrily.

She kicked at him. Punched him. Tried to bite at his hand.

He backed her up against the car until the weight of him restrained her movements. The evidence of how the fight excited him pressed against her and confused her even more. She questioned her survival instincts along with her sanity. There was nothing sexy about being held against her will, and yet her body was hot with hunger for him. Her sex was wet with need. Her nipples hardened against his strong chest.

"Don't look at me that way," he growled. "I'm trying to do the right thing."

She would have asked him what the hell that was but his hand still covered her mouth, so she kicked him as hard as she could.

He grunted and adjusted himself more fully against her so she didn't have the leverage for another strike. "I don't know why your uncle expected you to go along with this. Does he know you at all?"

She struggled against him, inadvertently moving her

stomach back and forth across his bulging cock. When she realized how her movements were actually exciting both of them more, she stopped.

He closed his eyes briefly, then said, "I'm going to take my hand off your mouth. If you start screaming I'm going to kiss you, and we both know where that will lead. Stop fighting me, because I'm not a knight in shining armor, and you've already got me revved half out of my mind. Calm down so I can."

She took a deep, calming breath and nodded once. He removed his hand slowly. "How could I possibly go along with this, when I don't know what *this* is?"

He also took a deep breath and straightened so she was no longer pinned beneath him. "I'm trying to rescue you, but you're making that fucking impossible."

ANDREW HADN'T GOTTEN to nearly thirty without ever being betrayed by his dick, but he'd assumed he was well past that stage. He wasn't a schoolboy accidentally dancing too close to a girl and involuntarily sporting an obvious boner. Men learned to control that shit. Okay, yes, when he'd sunken to the point where he'd needed a drink in the morning just to make it to the drinks he'd indulged in the rest of the day—he'd given his dick free rein. This was different, though. This was him sober, trying to remove a woman he was growing to like from harm's way, looking like an oversexed kidnapper. *Something I could talk myself out of if those big eyes of hers didn't reduce me to a bumbling idiot.*

Given a little space, she folded her arms across her chest

and looked up at him warily. "You must think I'm pretty gullible."

"No, I think you've got a lot of fight in you, considering you've lived a sheltered life. I understand how confusing this must be for you, but it doesn't change the reality of your situation. Your uncle asked me to get you back to your parents, and that's what I intend to do."

She narrowed her eyes at him. "I don't believe you, but pretend for a moment that I do. If my uncle didn't think I was safe here, why wouldn't he just tell me to leave? Why would he have someone like you *take* me anywhere?"

Someone like me. I can't even dispute her assessment that I'm the wrong man for this job. "He said he didn't know who he could trust."

Her eyes rounded in disbelief. "But he trusts you?"

Andrew sighed harshly and turned so he rested against the car. "Listen, I didn't go to dinner hoping to be flying you home tonight. I thought your uncle seemed like a nice guy. I was going to stick around long enough to make sure you were safe and then go back to my own crazy family."

She rolled her eyes skyward. "Keep me safe from what? I wasn't in any danger before you arrived."

"You may be right about that."

She shivered visibly. "Would you just tell me whatever or whoever it is that you think is out to get me? Because, frankly, I'm not sure anything or anyone could be scarier than you."

"I would tell you if I knew."

She raised one hand in a motion to stop. "Wait, you're

saving me, but you don't know who from?"

"I would know if you hadn't interrupted when your uncle was about to tell me."

Her mouth rounded in shock. "Interrupted? You were mauling him."

"We were talking." He hadn't planned to tell Helene anything her uncle had said, but she wouldn't leave with him unless she knew why she needed to. "He did something that he's afraid has put you, as well as him, in danger."

She put her hand up and waved for him to stop. "First, I don't believe that my uncle would turn to you for help. He doesn't know you. Second, I can't imagine my uncle doing anything besides helping people. So, let me tell you what I think really happened. You threatened my uncle. Maybe with your gun. I don't know. He said whatever he needed to, to get you to leave so he could call the police. They are probably out looking for us already. Any minute now we'll see them tracking my cell phone, and they'll haul you off to jail. If you don't touch me again, I'll suggest they go easy on you."

"If your uncle wanted the police called, he wouldn't have taken your phone. And he wouldn't have given it to me."

"Maybe he was afraid they'd be too late to arrive if I called then."

"So he sent you away with me? To buy time for them to arrive? Does that make sense? He *wanted* you to leave with me. Remember what he said? 'She's all yours.' Does that sound like someone who is rushing inside to call the authorities?"

She brought her hands to her ears. "No. Shut up. I don't know why he said that. I don't understand any of this."

Andrew turned on his hip so he was facing her. "He said it because he knows I care about you, and that I'll do whatever I need to do to get you back to your parents."

She shook her head and blinked back tears. "I don't know what to believe."

He turned her face gently toward his. "Look at me. Believe *me*."

"Who is my uncle afraid of?"

"I told you—I don't know, but he said involving you will put you in danger."

"Is it drugs? Gambling? Does he owe someone money?"

Andrew didn't answer.

She turned fully to face him. "I have a right to know. If you really think my uncle is in trouble, then I need to know how to protect him. He's my family. I'm not leaving without him."

Andrew's hands clenched at his side. He didn't want to say it, but maybe she did need the truth. "He killed my brother."

She gasped. "No. No, he didn't."

"He told me he did."

She searched his face. "He used those words? He said, 'I killed your brother'?"

"Not exactly. He said it was his fault."

She let out a shaky breath. "That's not the same."

To me it is. I carry the guilt of those who died because of my mistake. I killed them just as surely as if I'd rigged the box myself.

She pushed, "How? How did he say he caused it?"

"He didn't. He just said he was sorry. We didn't have a long heart-to-heart over it. He said he was in danger and begged me to take you back to Florida. You know the rest because you showed up."

She turned to face away from him, shaking her head. "Whatever happened to your brother was an accident. My uncle might feel guilty about it, but he would never do anything to harm anyone."

"I'm not so sure about that, Helene. A lot of people disappeared after my brother died. Their names are listed in my aunt's journal."

"Then maybe your aunt killed them, but my uncle never would." She brought a trembling hand up to her lips. "If my uncle was that horrible a person he wouldn't be afraid, would he? But if he's afraid, he's innocent."

"I don't know that one proves the other."

"It does to me. Take me to the clinic and I'll prove to you that my uncle did nothing wrong. I know where the records from that year are kept. They're all in boxes in the back of the file room. My uncle said he was looking for them, but he didn't know where they were. We could bring them to him, and he could prove his innocence."

"He made it sound like whoever was coming for him might come soon."

Her teary eyes flew to his. "And you left him?"

Andrew growled defensively, "He had just said he killed my brother."

"No, he didn't. He never said those words."

Andrew threw up his hands. "I give up. You want to stay and try to clear your uncle's name? Fine. You'll probably get him killed, along with you and me, but you know what? At this point, you're probably doing us all a favor." He opened the passenger door again. "Get in."

"Why?"

He left her there by the open door and walked around to the driver's side. "We can walk to the clinic if you want, but driving is faster."

She hastily climbed in the passenger seat and buckled herself in. "The files will clear everything up. You'll see."

He watched her muster a brave face, and his heart pounded loudly in his chest. She remained loyal to her uncle even through this shitstorm. Outside of the Corps, he couldn't remember ever having that kind of faith in anyone or anyone having that kind of faith in him. He wanted her to find something to clear her uncle, but he didn't believe for a second that she would.

Still, that didn't stop him from starting the car and heading toward the clinic.

Chapter Eight

HELENE USED HER name tag to open the front door of the clinic. The night security man recognized her and stood. "Ms. Franklin, I wasn't expecting anyone tonight."

"I wasn't expecting to be here." She spoke quickly thinking that everything would go a lot smoother if Andrew said as little as possible. "We were having dinner when my uncle realized he'd forgotten a box of old files he wanted to read through to decide if they should be shredded or added to the database. It could have waited until tomorrow, but you know my uncle. He likes things done right now. Family. They can't fire you, but you can't say no either, so here we are." She shot him a bright smile that softened the other man's expression.

"Of course. Tell me if you need me to help carry the box."

Helene linked her arm with Andrew and gave him a tug. "I brought my own muscle, thanks."

As she and Andrew walked down the hallway, Andrew whistled in appreciation. "You lie like a pro."

She shrugged and, not wanting to draw attention from

the security guard, forced herself to walk slowly. "I may not have traveled much, but that doesn't mean I'm an idiot. It's not like I could hide a year's worth of files under my shirt."

"I never said you were an idiot."

"You don't have to. I see it in your eyes. You think you're smarter than I am. You're not. And I'm going to prove it to you."

She could have sworn she heard him say, "I hope you do," but she wasn't sure. She told herself that his opinion of her was insignificant in the face of everything going on. *I should have told him I could do this part alone.* She had a feeling, though, he wouldn't have listened to her anyway.

He followed her through her office to the file room. She went straight to where she'd stacked the old file boxes. Since she hadn't known how to do much when she'd first started working in the records department, she'd spent a good chunk of time in the beginning simply organizing. The boxes before her were completely out of order and some were shoved sideways as if someone had returned them to the pile in a hurry. She looked for the boxes that would have been full of files from the year Andrew's brother died but didn't see them.

"They have to be here," she said, starting from one end of the pile of boxes and going over them again. "All of the other years are here. I don't remember any missing."

Andrew kept his silence beside her.

The sound of her office door opening and closing made Helene swing around. Andrew withdrew behind a stack of files and pulled his gun. He motioned for Helene to call out.

"Hello?" Helene said nervously. "Is someone there?"

The security guard appeared in the doorway. "Just me. I wanted to make sure you were able to get into the file room."

Helene forced a smile. "I did. Thank you."

The guard looked around. "Is your friend still with you?"

Andrew tucked his gun away again, quickly undid the buttons of his shirt, and mussed his hair before stepping out from behind the files. His grin was sheepishly guilty. He made a show of buttoning his shirt. "I am."

"Oh," the guard said and cleared his throat. "Well, I'll be at my desk if you have trouble locking up."

Helene met Andrew's eyes and understood how his ruse might buy them a cover story for being there longer. "Please don't tell my uncle."

"Of course," the guard said and turned on his heel, leaving with a haste that implied he wished he hadn't checked on them.

When he was gone, Helene returned to hunting for the box. Thanks to Dr. Gunder, everyone at the clinic already thought she was sleeping with Andrew. Her reputation there was also the least of her worries. After checking and rechecking the pile, she hunted through the more recent files. Eventually she stopped and went to her computer. She searched every area of the database for anything about the Barringtons, but there was nothing. Eventually she asked, "What was the name of the nurse you were looking for?"

"Pamela Thorsen."

"Nothing. There's nothing here about your family or her. Do you have any of the other names?"

He named two doctors, the one who delivered the babies and another who was on duty that night, but she couldn't find them either. Remembering what her uncle had said about not all the files being uploaded to the new database, she retrieved paper copies of random files from the years before and after. Everything from those files was in the database. Everything. She finally stopped typing in names and simply looked across at Andrew in confusion. "I don't understand. It's like your family was never here. There's no record of anyone you're looking for either. Are you sure you have the names right?"

"As certain as I am of anything in this mess."

"Someone is covering their tracks, erasing everything from that time."

"It looks that way."

"We have to tell my uncle."

Andrew crossed his arms across his chest. "I'm sure he knows."

Helene stood. "You think he's responsible?"

Andrew looked skyward as if appealing for help. "You don't?"

Anger swept through Helene. Andrew didn't know her uncle. He didn't know anything about him. She pushed past him and walked out of her office without bothering to close or lock any of the doors behind her. Andrew fell into step beside her. "Where are you going?"

She didn't answer him. She strode up to the security guard's desk and plastered a huge smile on her face. "You're not going to believe this, but I think someone already picked up the files we need. My uncle must have asked someone else to get them. Do you remember anyone leaving with a box of files recently?"

The guard shrugged. "No, but I work nights mostly."

She bit her bottom lip and feigned a pout. "My uncle will be so upset with me if I tell him I don't know where those files are. Is there anyone who would know?"

Andrew stepped forward. "Or is there a camera outside the office that you could review the footage?"

The guard reluctantly looked at the control panel in front of him. "How far back would I have to search?"

"Start with today," Andrew said smoothly.

"It's really important," Helene pleaded softly.

Grudgingly the guard pressed a few buttons and called up the feed from that camera. He scanned backward from their arrival and stopped. "I think I found it." He bent to study the video closer. "It looks like Dr. Stiles left with a box of something around seven."

Helene leaned over the counter. He had to be mistaken. "Are you sure? Are you sure it's my uncle?"

The guard gave her a look. "I would hope I can recognize the man who signs my paychecks."

Shock mixed with confusion and Helene swayed on her feet. Andrew put his hand on Helene's arm to pull her back from the guard's station. "Don't you hate when messages get confused? Helene, he probably told you that you don't have to pick up those files. You need to pay better attention."

"I guess," she said slowly, still trying to absorb the fact that her uncle had been late to dinner because he'd been at the clinic removing old files. He hadn't brought them with him into the house. Had he planned to? Was there a chance that he'd taken the files with the intention of showing them to Andrew?

Andrew began to lead her away and she stumbled. He placed his arm around her and said goodnight to the guard as they left the clinic.

My uncle took the files. Did he also wipe the computer? Why? What is he so afraid of?

She allowed Andrew to guide her back to his car and buckle her in. He didn't start the engine, though. He simply waited, looking at her with a mix of pity and something else in his eyes.

"Where's my phone?" she asked. He turned, found her purse in the backseat of his car, then handed it to her. She took out her phone and brought up her uncle's number. "I need to talk to him. If he took the files it was for a good reason. You'll see. We'll sit down with him, talk it out." She angrily used the back of her hands to brush the tears away from her cheeks. "He didn't kill your brother. I know he didn't. But he may be in some kind of trouble. If he is, will you help me help him?"

She hated that she had to ask anyone, never mind Andrew, for help, but her heart broke imagining her kind uncle alone and scared. No person, or creature, deserved that.

When Andrew didn't answer her, she turned in her seat to face him. "Please."

He started his car and ground the gears as he pulled out onto the road. She took his response as a yes and said, "I'm going to call him now, but head back to his house."

Andrew drove without giving any indication that he'd heard her, but when they came to the turn that would lead them back to her uncle's he took it.

With hands that were shaking so much she almost dropped her phone, Helene called her uncle and held her breath while it rang several times.

As THEY DROVE toward Stiles's home, Andrew reflected on what he'd said to her when she'd asked to be taken to the clinic. He'd said that she was probably going to get them all killed but that she'd probably be doing them all a favor. He glanced at the woman beside him. His gut twisted painfully at the idea of losing her. She not only had the fight of a Marine, but the loyalty of one, too. She had to be afraid, but she wasn't giving in to it. When he'd first met her he would have said it was because she was too innocent to comprehend the real danger they might be putting themselves in, but that wasn't it. She genuinely loved her uncle, and she wasn't leaving without him.

He wanted to grab the phone out of her hand, because he had a sinking feeling that when she spoke to her uncle her love for him would be tested in a whole new way. Stiles was an unknown risk Andrew wanted to forbid Helene to open herself up to, but there were some things in life that even a Marine couldn't protect someone from. She could no more walk away from her uncle than Andrew could have walked away from a firefight.

Her dedication to her family brought Andrew's emotions

to the surface. He realized he might have a second chance at his life. Exercising had brought his body back into shape, but it hadn't lifted the numbness that had made him indifferent toward his own survival. He hadn't gotten as far as holding a gun to his head, but he'd understood how a man could, and it hadn't scared him. He'd already felt mostly dead.

No matter what happened, he knew his life would forever be different because he'd met the woman beside him. She reminded him that true courage started in the heart; it was born in believing. She looked down at her phone; her uncle hadn't answered her call.

Her eyes flew to his and her tears returned. "He might not be near his phone."

Andrew reached out and took one of her hands in his, giving it a squeeze. For her, he would try to believe in possibilities. "Call again."

She sniffed, nodded, and did. This time her uncle did answer. She put him on speakerphone. "Uncle Clarence, are you at the house? We're driving back for you. You're not alone. We'll figure this out together."

"Where is Andrew?" her uncle asked hurriedly.

"He's beside me," she said, squeezing Andrew's hand. "He's willing to help you, too."

"Put him on the phone."

"He can hear you," Helene said.

"You should both be in the air by now. Why aren't you?" Stiles asked in a tight voice.

Years of taking orders made Andrew pause before he answered, but there was no chain of command here. "Your niece isn't quite as helpless as you seem to think she is. There was no way to take her without hurting her."

Helene chimed in, "We just left the clinic. I know you took files from it. Is someone blackmailing you? What kind of trouble are you in?"

"The clinic?" Stiles asked, his voice rising as he spoke. "You were supposed to be gone. Oh, my God. I can't go back now. Where are you?"

"We're almost at your house," Andrew answered. It was only then he noticed the street was blocked off and smoke was billowing up into the night sky.

"I'm not there," Stiles said in a high pitch. "You can't be there, either. Helene, all that matters now is your safety. Get out of Aruba. Now."

Andrew pulled over to the side of the road and instantly regretted that he had because Helene bolted out of the car and rushed down the street toward the emergency vehicles and fire trucks. He heard her cry out, "Your house is on fire."

"Andrew," Stiles yelled, "get her out of there."

"Who did this?" she asked from the middle of the road about one hundred yards away from the action.

"Your uncle set the fire. Didn't you, Stiles?" Andrew barked the question. "You're destroying the evidence against you."

With huge eyes, Helene looked from the burning house, to the phone, to Andrew, and back at the house. "What did you do, Uncle Clarence? What did you do?"

Her uncle's voice broke. "I was young, scared, and didn't

understand that when you make a deal with the devil it's forever. You won't hear from me after today, Helene. I have to disappear, or you'll never be safe. Everything that's burning in the fire had to disappear, too. Walk away from all of this. Go home. Tell no one about what you think happened here. Every single person you tell is someone you make a target. This is bigger than you know. Don't ask questions. Go home. Now."

Helene shook her head vehemently. "You didn't kill anyone. I won't let you destroy the proof that could clear you." She took a step toward the house, but Andrew grabbed her arm.

"Andrew, get her out of there. Helene, remember that I love you." With that, he hung up.

Helene tried to rip her arm away from Andrew, but he held her. "We have to go in there. There might be something left that will help him."

The woman beside him faded away, and for a moment Andrew was back in Iraq. Three of his Marines had just headed into a building to pick up a crate Colonel Ahearn had sent them for. One last mission before their tour ended and they headed home. Andrew was on watch on the street. He heard the explosion as if he were actually back in that horrifying moment. He was once again radioing in the incident, rushing into the building, coughing as the smoke burned at his throat. He fought to put out the flames that stood between him and the men he considered family. He hadn't allowed himself the luxury of feeling anything when he realized all three of them had fallen because the crate had been booby-trapped. There was no need to check if they were alive, the damage to each was irreversible. He assessed the dispersed contents of the box as he mentally planned how many trips it would take to get all three bodies back to his vehicle before the fire overtook them. It appeared to be a pilot seat from a MiG, which he left for last. By the time he went back for it, the room had been engulfed in flames and all he could do was watch it burn. A part of him had known the truth that day but hadn't been willing to accept it. He'd gone back to his Hummer, looked down at the tarp he'd covered the bodies of his friends with, and, on the inside at least, died along with them.

Helene's struggling brought him partially back to the present.

"Let me go," she demanded.

The past was just as much a part of that moment as her uncle's burning house. His hand bit into her arm. She wasn't going anywhere near that building. "No."

"I have to know if there's anything left of those files." She pulled harder, twisting with her whole body in an attempt to free herself. "You can't stop me."

"Yes, I can," he said harshly and began to haul her back toward the car.

"What is wrong with you?" she cried. "Everything I need to know is in there. For all we know, everything you came to find is in there, too. We can't just do nothing."

"Yes, we can," he ground out.

"No," she said, pulling back as hard as he was pulling forward. "I will not give up on my uncle. All he wants is for me to be safe. I don't believe he killed anyone. And I won't believe it unless I see hard proof, and it's in that house. You have to help me, Andrew. Help me get it."

He grabbed her by both arms, lifted her an inch off her feet, and shook her. "Let it burn. There is nothing in there worth your life or mine."

"You're hurting me," she cried out, and he came fully back to the present.

He instantly lowered her, released her arms, and pulled her to his chest. Shame. Fear. Guilt. It all gripped him as he wrapped his arms around her. Tears filled his eyes, and he hid his face in her hair. "I can't let you go in there, Helene. I'm sorry. I'm so sorry. I can't lose you, too." Emotions he'd held in for too long ambushed him, and he shook against her as tears silently ran down his face.

Chapter Nine

EELING ANDREW BREAK against her shifted her focus
from her uncle's pain to his. Several realities were
rammed home fast: she'd clung to the possibility that things
were not as bad as they seemed, but there was no longer a
way to deny that the danger was real. The fire before her was
proof of exactly how serious her uncle thought the threat to
them was.

Good or bad, criminal or unwilling accomplice, her uncle had run like a coward and that was difficult for Helene to
process. He may have asked Andrew to get her out of Aruba,
but he hadn't stuck around to make sure she was safe. The
man who was holding her had. The man who'd let her
glimpse his fear: *I'm sorry. I'm so sorry. I can't lose you, too.*

Helene wrapped her arms around his waist and hugged
him tightly. His sorrow was so intense she found herself
weeping with him. She cried for whatever happened to him
that had damaged him so deeply and the role she was playing
in making him face it again. *I'm such an idiot.*

She leaned back so she could see his face. "I'm sorry, too,
Andrew."

He shook his head and laughed without humor. "You're the only one in this shitfest who has done nothing to be sorry for."

She tenderly wiped the tears from his cheeks. "That's not true. You warned that I'd probably get us killed, and I wouldn't listen. I wanted to be right so badly that I wasn't thinking straight. We could have been on our way back to the States by now."

He smoothed her hair with his hand. "You couldn't leave your uncle."

"He didn't have a problem leaving me." She looked away and blinked back fresh tears.

Andrew didn't refute that, but what could he say? Her uncle was not only a coward, but he'd also admitted to having been the cause of the death of Andrew's brother. "You must hate me."

Andrew kissed her forehead and pulled her back into his arms. "If by hate you mean I want to carry you off and lose myself in that sweet body of yours all night, then yeah, sure."

She frowned up at him. "How can you think about that right now?"

He shrugged one shoulder, settled her more firmly against his excitement and asked, "How can you not?"

Passion flared through her even though she felt very close to disintegrating into tears. "You're crazy, do you know that?"

A slight smile curled one side of his mouth. "I've questioned your own sanity at least five time since we met, and it's only been a couple of days."

She chuckled without humor and turned her head so she could see her uncle's house. "What do we do now?"

He stepped back and took her hand in his. "Now I take you home."

She searched his face. "To my parents?"

An odd expression came and went on his face. "Of course."

Disappointment ripped through her, confusing her even more. *Of course. How else did I think this would end?*

They returned to his car and were well on their way to the airport before Helene spoke. "Where do you think my uncle is?"

"The world is a pretty big place when a man wants to hide."

She nodded, still trying to come to terms with how much had happened over the last few days. "What do you think will happen to the clinic and its patients?"

He switched gears. "It's not the only medical center on the island. We all think we're indispensable; we're not. The clinic will probably close, but life will go on."

"You're probably right."

"I am."

She hugged her arms around herself, feeling cold despite the warm air temperature. "I'm grateful to you, but I may start calling you Mr. Positivity."

"Do it and I'll call you . . . let's see . . . sugarlips."

"I'm sure my parents would love that." She froze as a thought occurred to her. "Are you going to meet them? I mean, once we get back to the States there won't be a reason for us to see each other, will there?"

He met her eyes briefly. "I'm not leaving your side until I'm sure you're safe."

She hugged herself tighter and tried not to think too much about how his words made her feel good and bad at the same time. They rode along in silence for a while, then she asked, "If you ever want to talk about what happened to you, I just want you to know I've helped many creatures overcome trauma."

"Creatures?" he asked in a slightly amused tone.

Helene bristled a little defensively. "I'm not joking. Animals experience pain, fear, and loss just as deeply as we do. We had this spider monkey once who had been brought into the United States illegally as a baby. When his owner died, he bounced around, getting more violent and out of control with each new home. By the time he came to us, the road back to trust was long, but we eventually reached him."

"Have you always been involved in animal rescue?"

"My parents started their rescue straight out of college. You could say I was born into it. I grew up bottle-feeding tiger cubs and treating injured animals. I almost became a veterinarian."

"What stopped you?"

She stared out the passenger window as she answered. "My family doesn't have a lot of money. Whatever came in went for the care of the animals and the upkeep of the rescue. There was a period of time, just about when I was heading off to school, when the rescue almost went under. My parents couldn't afford to pay someone to replace me if I left. I had to choose between saving the animals at the rescue or saving animals in the future. The choice wasn't easy at the time, but I don't regret choosing the rescue. We've successfully returned hundreds of animals to their natural habitat. There's so much wrong with the world that thinking about it can be overwhelming. I know I can't change everything, but whenever we have a success story I feel like I did something to tip the scales in the right direction." She glanced back at him. "You probably think that's silly."

His answer was to raise her hand to his lips and kiss it. "What happened to the monkey?"

She instantly wished she'd picked a different example. "Not every case has a happy ending. He did well for a while with us, then we sent him to an animal Primate Rehabilitation Center in Belize. They have a high success rate and are passionate about what they do. Spider monkeys are endangered so each one that can be returned to the wild tips the scales in the right direction. He was socialized with a troop he was given time to bond with. They worked on predator avoidance skills, tagged him, and released him."

"And?"

"He was eaten by something a couple of weeks later." Andrew coughed and Helene shook his hand in reprimand. "It's not funny. It was awful."

"I'm sure it was," he said in a serious tone, but one side of his mouth twitched as if he were suppressing a smile. "I'm just remembering your elephant story and wondering if you need help choosing inspirational examples."

"You're an ass," she said and pulled her hand free of his,

although she could see how he'd find humor in what she'd said.

"No, I'm an angry elephant."

The comparison instantly cut through her. "Don't say that. Don't ever say that." The edge in her voice surprised even her.

He took her hand again. "I'm sorry. I didn't mean to make light of something that's important to you."

She clung to his hand and looked out the passenger window again. He'd misunderstood what had upset her. She hated that she and her family hadn't been able to save the elephant, but she accepted that not every animal that came to them could be rehabilitated. It was a harsh reality she'd found a way to live with, but in that moment she understood how he'd felt when she wanted to run into the fire. The idea of losing Andrew, especially to his anger and sorrow, was more frightening than anything she'd faced in Aruba. She didn't know how to express that fear to him so she didn't. Instead she simply tightened her hold on his hand.

"I'm sorry," he said tightly.

Without turning away from the window, she said, "It's okay." What she wanted to say was, "It will be okay. I'll find a way to make it okay," but she was afraid that if they started talking about anything serious again she would break down into tears. *How could Uncle Clarence have left without knowing if I was safe? How do I even begin to be okay with that?*

They didn't speak for several minutes, until she couldn't bear the silence another moment. If something didn't change it would be a long, painful flight home. She forced a smile on her face and turned to look at him. "I prefer the nickname I came up with for you the first time we met."

He arched an eyebrow. "Should I ask?"

"Probably not."

A smile stretched his lips. "Is it a swear?"

She raised her chin playfully. "I'm not saying." He turned down a private road. "I thought we were going to the airport."

"Felipe Ambrosio has a home with an airstrip here."

"The race car driver?"

"Yes. He should have a plane we can use. I'll call him. If he doesn't, I'll have one here within the hour."

"People lend you their planes? Just like that?"

He gave her a sidelong look. "You don't know much about my family, do you?"

Helene remembered what her uncle had said about them. "I know they're wealthy."

He made a face. "To a repulsive degree. It defines who they are. I walked away from that life as soon as I was old enough. I go home only when I absolutely have to. There are, however, certain perks to being a Barrington. People tend to worry so much about trying to impress them, and therefore me, they forget they can say no when I ask for something."

Helene opened her mouth to say she wasn't impressed by money, but he brought the car to an abrupt stop in front of an enormous private home that was fully lit up against the dark night. Even though Andrew spoke of money as if it disgusted him, if the man who owned that house worried about impressing him, Andrew's life had very little in common with hers.

Which isn't a problem because all he promised was to stay until he knows I'm safe.

He let go of her hand so he could make a phone call, and she gave herself a firm mental smack. *I don't even really know this man. I was convinced he was kidnapping me earlier. If he actually gets me home, I should be grateful for that alone. The only reason he's here with me at all is that my uncle . . . No, I can't think about Uncle Clarence right now. I would have helped him if he'd let me. I just hope none of this makes the news back in the States, because I've never been able to lie to my parents, but if it keeps them from being involved in whatever Uncle Clarence did here, then I'll learn to.*

"All set," Andrew said. "Grab your purse; his pilot is meeting us on the airstrip."

"Right now? How is that possible?"

"He uses a local man."

"Who is free right this moment to fly us home?"

Andrew made a face as if he was revealing a side of himself he wasn't proud of. "As I said, people don't say no."

HALF AN HOUR later, Andrew poured a ginger ale and asked Helene if she would like something to drink. She looked like she would have welcomed something with a bit more of a kick, but he wasn't sure he could pour one for her without pouring one for himself.

What a day.

He hadn't allowed himself time to think too deeply about its twists and turns while he was in the middle of the insanity. He'd learned early that it was best to remain focused on the moment until the bullets stopped flying. Although none had physically been fired in Aruba, Andrew felt like a man who'd fought and lost again.

He was leaving Aruba without the answers his brother had sent him to find. He hadn't been able to help Helene's uncle and, if he was honest with himself, he wasn't sure how much he would have done if given the chance.

The only thing I did right was get Helene out of Aruba. And now I'm taking her home.

A woman whose uncle's actions forever changed my family. Not her fault, and something that happened before she was even born, but still, that's fucked up.

I'm fucked up.

Helene was reading a magazine, affording him an opportunity to study her profile. A wave of possessiveness washed over him. There was no way he was walking away from her when they reached Florida.

He shook his head at his priorities.

I should care more about how my brother died than about a woman I just met. Kent is dead, though. What do I do with the knowledge that it wasn't an accident? Tell my family? And then what? How will the truth help them? All it would do is rip open old wounds. And likely cause my mother to have another breakdown.

No.

Some men would vow revenge. They'd hunt Stiles down and

*make him pay. His death, though, won't bring my brother back.
I've killed too many people in the name of my country; I can't
handle more blood on my hands.*

*I can't wrap my head around this, though. What possible
reason could anyone have had to kill an infant? What kind of
person could do something that heinous? Had Stiles done it
himself or been part of the cover-up? And what was the link
between my mother's sister and Stiles? Why would a crime that
Stiles committed be recorded in her journal? It wouldn't be
unless she'd somehow been involved.*

Oh, yes, that would definitely send my mother over the edge.

He thought about Gabrielle. If the truth were what mattered most, he should tell her that her husband wasn't the
war hero she thought he was. It would ease his own guilt if
he told her what he suspected they'd actually been doing
there. How would she handle discovering that her husband's
death had only been honored because the colonel had needed
to make sure Andrew would have a reason to keep the truth
to himself?

His friends had died, not heroically trying to retrieve
classified materials. They'd died because the colonel had
wanted a trophy. They died for nothing. And they'd still be
alive if Andrew hadn't blindly accepted the colonel's orders.
He always studied the details of their missions, but they'd
been at the end of their tour and were feeling cocky.

*All I had to do was ask what was in the crate, but I charged
ahead like we were invincible.* What had Stiles said? "It
doesn't matter how much good we do before or after, we
never rise above our lowest moment."

Accurate for Stiles as well as for myself.

That's fucking depressing.

Helene looked up from her magazine and smiled at him. "You're staring at me. Do I have something on my face?"

He cupped a side of her face with one hand, gently caressed her cheek, then let his hand drop. "No, you're perfect just the way you are."

She gave him a funny look, then said, "You're just saying that so I won't kick you in the head again. It wasn't my fault, though. I thought you were going to kill me."

"You are a tough cookie to save. Worst damsel in distress ever." He chuckled.

She laughed lightly, then sobered. "I'm still in shock. I mean, none of this feels real. I keep expecting my uncle to call and say it was all a mistake, an elaborate joke." She sucked in an audible breath. "But he's not going to, is he?"

Andrew shook his head sadly. No, unfortunately, all of it was fucking real.

She chewed her bottom lip before saying, "I don't know what to tell my parents."

"Nothing. You heard your uncle. If you tell them anything, you put them at risk."

"They're all the way back in Florida. Do you really think whoever my uncle is afraid of would bother them there?"

Andrew's hands clenched. "We don't know what or who he was involved with."

She took a sip of her ginger ale. "I thought I wanted to know, but I don't anymore. What if I discover he really did hurt your brother? What would I do with that? Am I a coward if I don't actually want to face that?"

"You're not a coward, Helene; you're just more honest with yourself than most. You have no idea how much I wish he hadn't told me he was responsible for Kent's death. I don't know what to do with that either."

"Because of how it would hurt your family."

"Exactly."

"My mother thinks her brother is a wonderful man, just like I used to. How do I tell her there's a good chance he's a monster?"

"You don't."

"I just bury it? Pretend today didn't happen?"

It was a question he'd asked himself a hundred, no a thousand, times. She was looking to him for the answers he was still searching for himself. "It's all we can do."

"Is it?" She looked into his eyes for a long moment. "Maybe it is." She took another sip of her drink then swirled the ice in the cup. "My parents will want to know why I'm back. They don't need me anymore. I was supposed to go out and find myself. I'm coming home more lost than I left."

"So don't go back."

Her eyes flew to his. "I have to."

"Why?"

Her head tipped to one side as if she were explaining something that should have been obvious. "I haven't seen them in over a month. I've missed them more than I could express in words."

"You just said they don't need you anymore."

"That doesn't mean they don't love me and want me

there with them. My mother is my best friend. My father says something every day that makes me smile. I need them now more than ever. Are you really not like that with your family?"

He turned forward in his seat. "I told you, I only go home when I have to."

"Because they're horrible people?"

He sighed. "Not horrible, just very different than I am."

"So they're a meek, quiet bunch?" she asked dryly.

"Hardly."

"Lazy?"

"The opposite. I'd call most of them obsessively driven."

"How exactly are they different from you?"

After the day he'd had, the last thing Andrew wanted to do was delve into the issues he had with his family, but she was looking at him with those damn, expressive eyes of hers that made it impossible to deny her. "My mother took the death of my brother hard. She had a breakdown and after that it was all about being careful to not upset her. Everything came second to that. I was always wrong, always too much."

"So you just started avoiding them."

"I used to go home when my mother asked me to, but lately they're all so . . . too . . ."

"What?" Helene asked, leaning forward.

"Fucking happy."

"Assholes," she said wryly.

"Laugh, but you should see them. Everyone is either getting married, having a baby, or celebrating something."

She placed her hand on his arm. "Meanwhile, you're falling apart on the inside."

He looked down at her hand then placed his on it. Although there was nothing funny about how he felt, he tried to make a joke. "Which animal does that remind you of?"

Without missing a beat, she said, "We had a hedgehog once—" He looked up at her in surprise and she said, "Sorry. I'm just screwing with you. We don't have hedgehogs. I just wanted to make you laugh. My stomach is so nervous I feel like if I don't think about something else I may throw up."

"We could always focus on this." He took her chin in his hand, swooped down, and claimed her mouth with his.

Chapter Ten

I T MIGHT HAVE been a need to feel close to someone after the rollercoaster of a day she'd had, but Andrew's kiss felt as natural as heading home. She opened her mouth to him and welcomed his claiming. As much as he could be rough, Andrew could also be gentle. He teased her tongue in an intimate dance with his that sent desire rocking through her.

She didn't notice when he undid her seat belt, but he broke off the kiss long enough to lift her sideways onto his lap. He supported her with an arm behind her back and dug his other hand into her hair. She wrapped her arms around his neck and kissed him with an intensity that made every concern dissolve away. In that moment, she wasn't sad, tired, or confused. She was hungry for him and the pleasure his touch brought.

He caressed her neck then slid his hand down to cup her breast. "Oh God, Helene, you feel so damn good."

She tipped her head back, arching her neck as he kissed his way down it. "You do, too."

His hand tightened in her hair and he raised his head. "We need to stop. It's too good. I don't want to lose my head."

A woman could only be so careful, wait for so long. Helene didn't know what would happen when they landed in Florida. He said he wasn't leaving, but she couldn't blame him if he changed his mind. They had nothing in common, and essentially, her family had wronged his, but that didn't stop how much she wanted him. They had a couple hours before they landed. *I'm done waiting for the right time with the right man. I'm twenty-six. What if that time never comes? What if no other man ever makes me feel this way?* "Don't you dare stop," she whispered. "Don't you dare."

His eyes burned with need, and he gave her a pained look. "Are you sure?"

Her answer was to pull his mouth back to hers. It was all on then. He picked her up, carried her to the back of the plane, kicked the partially open door to a small bedroom out of the way, then closed it behind them. When he lowered her back to her feet he kissed her with a passion she'd always dreamed of. She met him with a need that matched his.

They tore at each other's clothing, moving to a standing position when they needed to. Her dress hit the floor, followed by her panties and bra. His shirt, pants, and boxers joined the pile. All the while, they never stopped kissing and exploring each other's body feverishly. He backed her up against the vanity and kissed her neck thoroughly before moving lower. She held on to the edge of the counter, gasping his name.

His cock nudged against her, and she reached for it. It was huge and hard. She was torn between wanting to feel it inside her right then and begging him to keep kissing her breasts the way he was. She moved so her feet were wider apart and cried out with pleasure when his hand found her sex. His fingers were strong and sure. He sought her clit and raised his head long enough to watch her reaction as he caressed it. When his rhythm had her begging him not to stop, he began to kiss her neck again. She stroked his cock, but he moved her hand off him. "This is about you, Helene. Let me make it good for you. Just relax and let me love you."

Who would argue with that?

He dipped his middle finger inside her, all the while caressing her clit with an expertise that blew her mind. He nipped at her breasts gently, sucked her nipples until she was wildly bucking against his hand. He worshipped her body with his mouth, all while stroking her intimately.

"Come, Helene. Come for me," he growled against her neck.

She did and it was beyond anything she'd expected. Wave after wave of heat shot through her, leaving her panting and shaken. "I had no idea," she whispered.

He moved and slid a condom on himself. "We're nowhere near done."

"Thank God."

There was no fear, only anticipation. He picked her up and carried her to the bed. He set her on it and sank to his knees between her legs. She'd thought his fingers were talented, but the way he worked her clit with his tongue had her digging her hands into his shoulders. His tongue slid deep inside her as he brought his thumb to her clit before his tongue returned to her nub. She could feel heat rising within her again. He guided her onto her back and poised himself above her.

"I don't want to hurt you," he said. "Tell me if anything is too much."

She nodded hastily, focused only on how much she wanted him inside her. He dipped his tip inside, then pulled it out and ran it along her wet sex before dipping in her again. She spread her legs wider and moaned as he kissed his way from her shoulder to her chin. It was torture waiting.

When he finally thrust inside her there was no discomfort, just a brief tightness. He moved slowly in and out, so gentle she wanted to punch him. She met his thrust with her own, wanting to feel him deeper. He took the hint, and there was more power in his next thrust.

"Oh, yes," she whispered. "Harder, Mr. Muscles. I want it harder."

"Fuck, yes," he said, and his gentleness fell away. She knew exactly when he let himself go because his moves were more passionate than planned. He pounded into her, and Helene clung to him as a second orgasm rocked through her.

He kept going through her orgasm until he finally gave in to his own with a swear. For a moment, his weight rested on her before he adjusted himself so he was poised above her. "I tried to be—"

She pulled his mouth to hers for a kiss, then in a ragged voice said, "It was amazing."

He turned, disposed of the condom, then pulled her into his arms. It had been everything and more than Helene had dreamed it would be. She was in heaven.

His arms tightened around her. "I didn't mean for this to happen."

She closed her eyes. "Shut up, before you ruin it."

He gave her ass a light slap. "Did you just tell me to shut up?"

She opened her eyes and met his. "I waited a long time for this. Let me savor this feeling. I don't want to think about anything else yet."

"I just want you to know that when we get to Florida—"

She placed her hand over his mouth. "Do you have another condom with you?"

He studied her face. "I thought you might need to talk."

She shook her head. "Do you?"

A lusty smile spread across his face. "No, I don't." He rolled so she was sprawled on top of him. "I am officially shutting up."

ANDREW WOKE TO Helene cuddling close to him and caressing his chest lightly. He kept his eyes closed and his breathing deep and steady. They'd made love twice, the second time had been less hurried and had left them both sated and sleepy. If she wanted to explore him as he slept, he didn't mind one bit. In fact, it was a pleasure beyond what he'd experienced with other women. Somehow, despite the insanity of how they'd come together, it felt right to have her at his side. He couldn't explain it, nor did he want to try. All he wanted was to continue to feel her hands stroke him, anywhere and everywhere she wanted. He groaned as he imagined them wrapped around his cock again.

"Andrew?" Her hand stilled.

He didn't budge.

"Mr. Muscles, are you awake?" she asked, and he couldn't help it, he smiled. Was that her secret nickname for him? If so, he approved.

He rolled over so his upper half was above her. "Guilty as charged." He took a moment to soak in the simple beauty of her before kissing her briefly. The desire he'd felt for her the night before was still there, but their connection felt deeper. He was used to waking to a woman in his bed. He'd liked some enough to let them stay as long as they pleased. He'd never been the type to throw a woman out, and had never needed to. Women who chose to be with him had always understood he wasn't the type to stay. There'd always been another deployment looming that brought all of his relationships to a natural end. His partners hadn't asked him for more, and he hadn't offered it. Promises were for people who believed in them, and he'd stopped promising a long time ago. His father's lack of fidelity had shaped his view of committed relationships. Beyond the Corps, he didn't put much faith in anything or anyone. Losing Lofton and the others had shaken even that.

The thing about Helene, the most terrifying part of being with her, was how easy it would be to believe in *her*. The sex had been phenomenal, but he wanted more from her. He wanted to be the one to protect her, the one to make her smile. He wanted to walk away from everything that was wrong with his life and lose himself in the goodness of hers.

She traced a small scar on his chin. "What were you going to tell me earlier?"

He ran his hand through her hair. "When?"

"You'd started to say something about when we get to Florida."

He tapped her nose lightly. "You mean just before you told me to shut up?"

She blushed. "Yes."

He loved the blush, loved that she could flip from brazen to sweet so quickly. "I was probably going to say some stupid shit I hoped would make you feel better about this."

She looked up at him intently. "You don't have to. I'm okay."

"Okay?"

She wrinkled her nose. "I'm not sixteen with expectations that this means anything. We both went through an emotional day. Two healthy adults in their prime. It was natural for us to find comfort in each other."

He frowned, not liking how easily she dismissed the time they'd spent bringing each other pleasure. "So, you would be perfectly okay if we parted ways when we land in Tampa?"

She tensed beneath him, but said, "Yes. I know you said you'd stay with me until you were sure I'm safe, but I will be as soon as I'm back with my family. You don't have to meet them unless you want to."

"I'm meeting your parents," he said firmly.

She gave him a curious look. "You can. I just didn't want you to think you have to."

He wanted to shake her and tell her that she'd just given

him her virginity; she had a right to have expectations. It had meant something to him, and he wanted to believe it meant something to her. His reaction took him by surprise. He sat up and looped his arms around his knees. "I'm definitely meeting your parents."

His tone seemed to make her uncomfortable. She pulled a sheet up to cover herself. "What I'm trying to say is that I don't want you to."

His jaw went slack, and he stared down at her in surprise. He had never been the man a woman was embarrassed to bring home. Hell, he and his brothers were consistently featured in magazine lists of the world's most eligible bachelors. "Why the hell not?"

She held the sheet to her chest. "You and I . . . all of this . . . I understand that it isn't going anywhere, but my parents will start hearing wedding bells just because I've never brought a man home before. I'm confused enough without trying to explain you to them." She smiled and joked, "Although they might be relieved to know I finally had sex with someone besides myself."

He didn't laugh and her smile turned pained. He liked her joking about their intimacy even less than he'd liked her dismissing it.

They looked at each other in an awkward standoff until she said, "I hate it when you do that."

"What?"

"Stare at me instead of sharing what you're thinking. Whatever it is, isn't it better to say it than keep it in?"

"Not in my experience." Her philosophy was the polar

opposite of how his family had always functioned. Most thoughts, especially those that might be controversial in any way, had always been kept silent. In his personal life, as well as his chosen profession, he was used to being told that his feelings came second to the good of the whole. "When it comes to what I actually think about most things, I do better if I keep my mouth shut."

She moved to a sitting position, still holding the sheet to her chest. "Now that surprises me."

"Why? Because I've lost count of how many people I've killed? There's no talking involved in taking someone out from a thousand yards away."

Her eyes rounded. "I was going to say because you come from a family of influence."

He groaned. *What a dumbass thing to say. She finally thinks I'm not dangerous and I say shit like that?* He cursed himself for giving in to the temptation to test her reaction.

She was silent for a moment then said, "Do you really not know how many people you've killed?"

He met her eyes. "I know exactly how many. It's not something a person forgets. I remember every face, every fall. I'm haunted by when I did it well *and* when inaccuracy made them suffer. I tell myself each was necessary, but how the hell do I know? They often don't say why. You have to trust they would only send you in if there was no other choice."

She laid a hand on his back. "I'm sorry."

He shook his head in self-disgust. "That's why I keep most thoughts to myself."

She shifted closer and rested her head on his shoulder. "You don't have to with me. I realize it's not the same, but running a rescue has made me familiar with the underbelly of humanity. Just like not every animal can be saved, not every person can be reasoned with. I've never taken a life, but I know what it's like to stand between the defenseless and a monster who would hurt it for no other reason than they can. Monsters exists, but you're not one, Andrew. You did what you did to defend our country. That doesn't make you a monster, it makes you a hero."

He turned and pulled her into his arms. "Not everyone would agree with you."

"Who gives a shit about them?" she asked, wrapping her arms around him.

He chuckled. *This. This is what I've never had. An . . . equal.* Someone who urged him to talk and then listened when he did. Someone the truth didn't scare. It was refreshing to be with her, refreshing to be himself. He sobered. "I want to meet your parents, Helene. You can tell them anything you want about us. I've never been a flowers and poetry kind of guy, but I need to say something. Maybe this ends in a day or a week. I don't know. All I know is I'm not ready for it to end now."

"I'm not either." She dropped the sheet and moved so she was in front of him, straddling his legs. She placed her hands on his shoulders and leaned forward to kiss him. Her excited nipples brushed over his chest as her wet sex slid over his quickly hardening shaft. He checked the clock beside the bed. They still had time before they reached Tampa.

Good.

He didn't have another condom, but there were other ways they could please each other. A Marine was always prepared to adapt, improvise, and overcome. He lifted her so she was on her feet, straddled before his face, and began to happily improvise.

Chapter Eleven

I T WAS LATE the next morning by the time Helene and Andrew drove their rental car down a long dirt road that led to the chain-link gate of the Free Again Rescue and Sanctuary. Helene told Andrew the code and the gate swung open for them.

She wasn't surprised to see both her parents sitting on the porch waiting for them. She'd called them soon after the plane had landed and had been vague about the reason for her return. They sounded worried until she said she had someone with her who she wanted to introduce to them.

"Is it a man?" her mother had asked, her pitch rising with excitement.

"Yes," Helene had said, grateful at the time that Andrew had stepped away to make a few calls of his own.

"I told you, Art," her mother had said. "I told you she would meet someone. She just had to get out there in the world."

She'd heard her father say, "Put her on speakerphone. Who is this guy, Helene? Why is this the first we hear of him?"

"It was kind of sudden, Dad."

"Art, don't you dare scare this one off," her mother had warned.

"Are you still harping on her prom date? All I did was ask him to hold my rifle while I found the bullets. I was kidding," her father had said. "But don't worry, had I known how few men would come around, I would have been nicer to even that wimp. I'll tone it down for this one."

Oh, God. Even as she started to worry about what her parents would say in front of Andrew, she told herself to be realistic. She and Andrew weren't in a relationship. They'd shared a batshit crazy day, had sex, and he'd said he wasn't ready for it to be over yet. *It* might have referred to simply sleeping with her. He was honest enough to say he didn't know if it would last a week or even another day. Although the idea of never seeing him again made her feel a little sick, she couldn't hate him for it. He'd stayed to protect her when a member of her own family had deserted her. He hadn't taken advantage of her. She'd wanted every single moment of being with him. If it wasn't meant to last, she'd find the strength to let him go. He had enough pain tearing him apart. She wouldn't add to it. In fact, no matter how things ended between them, she wanted to leave him better than how she'd found him in some way. Sometimes that's all a person could strive for. "You won't have to, Dad, he's a Marine."

"Nice," her father had said. "Enlisted or retired?"

"Where did you meet him?" her mother had asked.

Only because Helene didn't know if Andrew was between deployments or out for good, she chose to answer her mother's question. "At the clinic. He came in one day."

"Is he—?" her father started to ask.

"Does your uncle—?" her mother asked at the same time.

Helene hadn't been ready to answer their questions yet. "Can't talk now, but I wanted you to know that we'll be there in a couple of hours. See you in a few. Love you."

"Love you, too," they'd both answered.

To reduce the number of questions she and Andrew would face, they made a quick stop at the mall to buy a couple of outfits along with some luggage. They rented a hotel room for the night but stayed just long enough to shower and change. Everything that had happened with her uncle still felt unreal so she put it out of her mind even though inside her heart she ached. Despite how little time she might have with Andrew, or perhaps because of it, she chose denial over the craziness of reality. When she did, the time with Andrew was amazing. It was super charged with both sexual tension and the glow of a new friendship. Out of nowhere, he would say something that had her laughing until her sides hurt. At other times, he'd look at her in a way that had her melting at his feet and wondering how many times a day a person could have sex.

Unlike the men she'd known in the past, his attention to her was unwavering. She was quickly becoming addicted to the feel of his gaze on her or the touch of his hand caressing her.

Still, looking at her parents' faces reminded her that

nothing was as good as she was pretending it was. Not Aruba, not her relationship with the man beside her. She and her parents had always had an open and honest relationship.

"You look nervous," Andrew said.

She made a face and shook her head. "This was a bad idea." Before she had time to explain, her parents were standing beside her car door, waving at both of them, with embarrassingly huge smiles on their faces. Helene forced a smile and waved back as she said, "I've never been able to lie to them."

Andrew gave her hand a squeeze. "Take a page from my book then and simply say less."

Helene nodded. Her parents were dancing like puppies beside the car. "Before we go out there, I need to prepare you."

Andrew seemed to size her father up. They were about the same height, but her father had a good thirty years on Andrew. He looked back at her in confusion. "For what?"

"They *will* hug you."

She stepped out of the car. "Mom. Dad. This is my friend, Andrew."

ANDREW THOUGHT HELENE had been joking about her parents until her mother gave him a longer and tighter hug than he'd ever received from his own mother. He was still recovering from it when her father thanked him for his service and pulled him in for a back-slapping embrace that caught him off guard. They were both remarkably strong for their age.

Helene intervened. "Okay, Dad."

Her father smiled at Andrew and punched him in the arm. "Solid. You did good this time, Lenny." He lowered his voice as if by doing so the women couldn't hear him. "You could floss your teeth with the last man she dated."

"Lenny?" Andrew mouthed silently to Helene and fought back a grin.

Her mother said quickly, "Who she dated in the past doesn't matter. They're gone and forgotten. We're just glad she met someone."

Andrew glanced at Helene again. She looked embarrassed, and he wished there was a way to reassure her. He liked her parents. It was obvious they loved their daughter and wanted her to be happy. His family was all about keeping things perfect so they didn't share how they felt about most things. They had no clue when it came to their children's private lives, relationships or dating habits. In general, they preferred to not know. At least, that had always been the case before Kenzi had rocked the family with the revelation that she'd been raped. According to Kenzi, the family was now gathering often for game nights and opening up to each other. He couldn't imagine it.

He put his arm around a blushing Helene and pulled her to his side. "I stole her away from a man like that in Aruba. Should I worry that I'm not her taste?"

Helene dug her elbow into his side. "He's so funny."

"How long are you two here for?" her father asked.

Helene tensed. "I'm back for good if that's okay. Aruba was a nice vacation, but I belong here."

Her mother looked instantly concerned. "Oh, honey, you know you're always welcome here. I'm surprised my brother didn't call me. Did something happen?"

There was a delay before Helene shook her head. "He was probably too busy. No need for him to call. I just missed you."

Her father brought a hand to his chin and rubbed it. He was more reserved as he addressed his next question to Andrew. "What about you, Andrew? What are your plans?"

It touched Andrew that they wanted their daughter to settle down and were ready to accept him if he said that was what he wanted, too. They didn't know a thing about him, though. He thought about how far he'd let himself sink when he first left the Marines and wondered if they'd welcome him if they knew who he'd been then. Helene didn't lie to her parents and he decided he wouldn't, either. "I recently finished a tour in Iraq and decided not to reenlist. I'm from Boston, not Aruba, but I'm not anxious to go back there, either. I don't actually have a plan for what to do next."

Her father nodded. "How long were you in?"

"Twelve years."

Her father relaxed. "It's normal to not know what to do when you get out. You'll find your footing." He shared a look with his wife, then said, "Until then, you're welcome to stay with us as long you don't mind that we all pull our weight here. If you can't stomach the idea of cleaning out an animal pen, there's a hotel a few miles away."

Her mother added, "Not everyone likes animals, Art.

There's also work to be done that doesn't require getting quite so up-close and personal with them. We have fences to mend. Equipment that always needs a tune-up. We're hoping to start tours in the fall so we're slowly building a welcome facility as well. You could help with that if you're handy with a nail gun."

Andrew looked to Helene for some sign of what she wanted from him, but her expression was carefully neutral. "If Helene is comfortable with me being here, I'll help out wherever I'm needed."

Helene's eyes shone with emotion that she blinked away as she searched his face. "If you want to stay here, I'm okay with it."

Okay with it. She sure knew how to keep a man humble.

Her mother clapped her hands together. "That's settled then. You could both stay in the first-floor guest room instead of Lenny's. The guest room has a full-size bed."

Andrew's eyes flew to her father's. "I'm fine with the guest room by myself. Or if you have a bunkhouse or something I could stay there."

Her father nodded in approval. "You're going to work out just fine here."

Her mother wagged a hand at them. "Art, they're not children. Do you really want them sneaking around trying to copulate between the animal pens? There's no reason to make a big deal out of something that is perfectly natural."

Art grunted. "You're right. We don't have separate housing for employees because until recently, this has been a strictly family run rescue. Lenny's room is upstairs with us. I guess we don't want her falling down the stairs because she feels she has to creep around in the dark to see you."

Helene covered her face with her hand. "Please stop. You're embarrassing me."

Her mother stepped closer. "Honey, there's no need to be embarrassed. You're an adult, and we're happy for you. We just want you to know that you don't have to sneak around. Now that we have employees, we've been putting up surveillance cameras and neither of us wants to accidentally see that."

Her mother's calm explanation coupled with Helene's mortification made it impossible for Andrew to keep a straight face. "I'll leave that decision to *Lenny.*"

Helene looked up at him then across to her parents. "Separate rooms are fine."

There was a brief, awkward pause then her father said, "How about I help you bring the luggage in, Andrew? Then I'll give you a tour if you're interested."

"I'd like that." Andrew gave Helene a quick squeeze then left her to open the trunk of the car. After handing the smaller bag to her father, he turned in time to see Helene talking to her mother. He couldn't hear them but read her lips easily.

Her mother said, "Of course we're okay with him being here. You have a good head on your shoulders. If you like him, that's a good enough endorsement for us."

"Twelve years. That's a long time," her father said, drawing Andrew's attention back to the task at hand.

Andrew turned to follow her father to the house. "Yes,

sir."

"Call me Art. Everyone does. It's short for Arthur, but anyone who calls me that doesn't know me well enough to know I hate it."

"I'll remember that, Art."

Art led the way into the house and to the downstairs bedroom. "The sheets are clean and there are more pillows in the chest in the corner if you want them."

"Thank you," Andrew said, placing his bag down next to the bed.

"I'll run Helene's bag upstairs then meet you in the kitchen."

"Sounds good."

"One more thing," her father said.

Andrew turned to fully face him. "Yes?"

"That's my baby girl out there. If you hurt her, all your military training won't save your ass when I come for it. I'm happy to have you here, but I'm not afraid of prison if you give me a reason to kill you. We clear?"

"Yes, sir—Art. We're clear." There were men who would make a threat they had no intention or ability to follow through on. Art was not one of those men. His gaze was steady and there was no question he meant every word. Only a fool would dismiss him as an unworthy adversary. Art didn't rely on money or status to protect his family. He had strength of character and that realization completely won Andrew over.

"Good." With that, her father walked out of the room.

While waiting for him to return, Andrew checked out

the rooms he came across while looking for the kitchen. It wasn't a fancy home, but it was of decent size, furnished in a comfortable, practical style. The walls were covered with photos of Helene from all stages of her life. He smiled at some he was certain she wished weren't on display, but he loved what they said about what her family valued. His family displayed professional photos that were staged and flawless. These photos were snapshots taken under very different circumstances. They were *real*.

In all the photos she was either in jeans or shorts and a dirty T-shirt. Her hair was wild in some, in others pulled back in a ponytail that looked about to come undone. She always had an animal with her. Large, small, hurt, healthy— she stood proudly with them. He stopped when he came across a photo of her in front of the elephant she'd described. She was placing hay for him and seeming to encourage him to take it. It had Andrew scanning the wall for a photo of her with the monkey. When he found it, he was deeply moved by the love evident in her face while interacting with the animal.

Art spoke from behind him. "That photo makes Lenny a little sad. We keep it to remind her that although things don't always turn out the way we want, it doesn't make what we do less important. We partnered up with a hospital in Willomore, South Africa to return him to the wild. Not every animal can transition back. The ones who clearly can't stay here get placed in other sanctuaries that try to keep them safe and comfortable for the rest of their lives. Ideally, though, wild animals deserve the chance to return to their natural habitat. We work to give them that opportunity. Sometimes we fail, but I can't imagine doing anything else."

"Helene shared his story with me." He looked briefly at the other wall. "The one about the elephant, too."

Art came to stand beside him. "That one really hurt her. She wanted so badly to be part of the transition over, but we couldn't afford to send her. I keep that photo up to remind myself that sometimes things are important enough to find the money. I should have sent her. She needed to be there, regardless of the outcome."

Andrew pocketed his hands in his jeans. It was one thing to believe Helene and her family were good people, but quite another to witness it up close. He'd already contacted two of his old Marine buddies who were in the area and hired them to unobtrusively watch over the Franklins. In a similar fashion to how he'd felt when he'd first met Helene, he wanted to protect her parents.

Art gave Andrew a pat on the shoulder. "Ready to go see what we do here?"

Andrew nodded and followed him back out of the house.

Chapter Twelve

SCRUBBING OUT WATER buckets was second nature to Helene. She found comfort in the familiar chore. Nothing in her life here had prepared her for the depth of disappointment she felt each time she thought about her uncle.

Each time she circled back to what her uncle might have done, she wondered how Andrew could look at her and not hate her. If he had informed his family about what he'd learned in Aruba, he hadn't said anything to her. Like her, was he taking after an ostrich and hiding his head in the sand for as long as he could? Eventually they'd have to face the ugly reality of what had brought them together, but Helene was okay with delaying that day if he was.

She turned to reach for another bucket and saw Andrew leaning against a tree, watching her. She sprayed an arc of water over his head. "That's what you get for sneaking up on me."

He wiped his face, straightened, and started toward her. "Not sneaking, just appreciating the view. You sure you want to start a water fight with me?"

Playfully, she sprayed the grass a foot or so in front of his feet. "Since I'm the one with the water hose, yeah, maybe I do."

He was beside her with a speed that would have scared her if she'd seen it from any other creature on the rescue. One of his hands closed over hers on the nozzle of the hose. His other hand swept behind her and pulled her forward and flush against him. "What do you say now?"

Heat seared through her, and she dropped the hose to the ground. "I surrender?" she joked.

He kissed her as if every moment they'd been apart had been as hard on him as it had been on her. She threw her arms around his neck and gave herself over to the way he made her feel. The kiss went on and on but stayed controlled. Not even the wild hunger he lit in her was enough to rip off her clothing or his if there was a chance they were on camera.

He eventually raised his head and tucked her beneath his chin. "I needed that."

"Me, too," she confessed against his chest. They stood there, simply breathing each other in for a few minutes. Eventually Helene cringed and said, "About my parents earlier . . ."

He looked down at her. "Don't apologize for them. They're wonderful. Your father gave me a tour of the property. It's quite impressive. I was expecting to see small enclosures, but the southern area is more like an African savanna."

"That's how the rescue got its name. My parents believe

that every wild animal craves to be free again, so they give each of them as much as it can handle."

"Your father showed me the welcome center they're building. He said his dream is to run educational programs and open the entire rescue to the public."

"That's been his dream for a long time, but all of that takes money. He's been dabbling in social media to bring awareness to the rescue, though, and it has been working. My mother said they've even brought in some interns from the University of South Florida who believe in the rescue's mission. They've implemented some of their ideas and are making money from videos they've put on the Internet. Not sure how it all works, but they say they're gaining a huge following." She sighed. "You were right about voids filling in. They're happy I'm back, but they don't need me." He stepped back and pocketed his hands. Clearly he was thinking something and keeping it to himself. She met his eyes. "Say it."

He looked back at her wordlessly.

She threw a hand up in the air. "You probably agree with my mother. I shouldn't see this as a bad thing. It's an opportunity. I don't have to stay here. I can go anywhere. Do anything. I'm free."

He held his silence.

Helene began to pace in front of him. "It should be exciting, shouldn't it? Well, it's not. It's terrifying. I tried leaving, and look how that turned out. Life makes sense to me here. What we do makes sense. I'm trying, but I can't begin to understand what we learned in Aruba. I don't know how I'm supposed to feel about any of it. Angry? Guilty? Sad for everyone involved?" She swallowed hard, stopped, and met his eyes again. "I keep flipping back and forth between being grateful to have this time with you and guilty that my family had anything to do with hurting yours."

He pulled her back into his arms, and she could feel his heart beating wildly in his chest. "You have nothing to feel guilty for."

"It doesn't feel that way," she said. There was something she had to ask him, something she'd thought about only since she'd been home. "I've been thinking. I don't think my parents know anything, but we can ask them. My uncle might have said something to them."

He frowned. "No. It's not worth the risk."

She caressed his strong jaw. "You deserve to know what happened to your brother."

"It doesn't matter anymore. He's dead. My family has moved on. Even if we found out the truth, it wouldn't change anything. What I want has nothing to do with the past."

She searched his face. "What do you want?"

He looked away for a moment, then back. "To feel something. I want to care about something again. I lost that." His hands gripped her arms tightly. "I don't know if I'll ever be the man I was, but when I'm with you I want to be."

She hugged him tightly, forcing herself not to cry for him. He didn't want her pity. Like every other creature on the rescue, he was looking for hope. "Then you've come to the right place." She stepped back and took him by the hand. "I want you to see something."

He fell into step beside her.

As he followed her, he wasn't sure what to expect. So far the tour of the facility had been eye-opening. When he'd first heard that her parents had an exotic animal rescue, he imagined people who collected dangerous animals for the thrill of it. What he was discovering was that very few of the animals on the rescue stayed. The Finally Free Rescue and Sanctuary was more of a transitional place for animals on their way to a better place. Art had explained that most of their work, outside of caring for the animals while they were there, was in building relationships with agencies from all over the world who had the resources to get these animals out of Florida and as close to where they belonged as possible. Sometimes it was an animal preserve in their native country or a permanent home somewhere safe, but everyone celebrated when animals were able to go one step further and reintegrate back into the wild. Art said that around the globe more people were beginning to see reintegration as achievable where they once hadn't. A handful of failures shouldn't close off the opportunity for thousands of potential successes. He was committed to helping prove that.

She stopped in front of a large enclosure. "Although we do get all sorts of exotic animals, mostly we receive native animals who have been struck by vehicles. Everything from owls to alligators, bobcats to turtles. We've raised awareness in the surrounding communities so that people feel comfortable calling us when they see something. Many local veterinarians don't charge us for their services because they know the fate of the animals if no one steps in. This is the less flashy side of what we do, but it brings me joy on a regular basis. These animals haven't been handled by people. Returning them to the wild takes less time and has a higher rate of success. If you really do want to help out here, I'd start with these. Everyone wants to help a tiger when one comes through, but these guys are harder to rally the public's support for. Less flash means less money, but every life here is equally valued. The panther in this enclosure is two years old."

"I don't see him."

She nodded and waved at the expanse of fencing. "That's because this is a pre-release area. He's tagged with a locator so we know he's in there, but we don't want him to get used to people because he'll need to avoid them to survive. There was a time when the near extinction of panthers in Florida was considered a good thing. It's now Florida's state animal, and still one of the most endangered mammals on earth. We work with schools and local agencies to educate the population on the importance of keeping them in the eco-system. They keep the wild hog population down. Without them, deer, raccoons, rabbits, and other small mammals overpopulate and begin to stress the food supply. Nature has amazing, built-in checks and balances. We're fighting to help preserve that balance."

On the other side of the enclosure a tawny brown cat leapt from one large rock to another. He bared his teeth. The idea of her working with such an animal made Andrew uncomfortable. "You go in there?"

"Not unless he's tranquilized," she said with a small laugh. "My parents stressed to me early on that these animals are not pets and we shouldn't treat them as if they are. We've found an area south of here where females have been sighted and that's where he's headed. After that, my involvement will be with farmers there."

"In what way?"

"I'll help them write grants to fund purchasing motion-detection cameras and predator-deterring fencing to use when they have young calves needing protection. Ideally, the fencing won't be used year round. To survive, a panther requires an average territory of two hundred square miles. We really can co-exist with these animals if we have a plan. Rotating predator fencing protects livestock while allowing the panthers to hunt as they were born to."

There was a thoughtfulness to the entire process that was beautiful beyond what Andrew could find the words to express. The rescue explained so much of what he admired in her. She was strong because she needed to be. The work they did was not for the faint of heart. The loyalty she'd shown for her uncle had been learned here with her parents and their shared commitment to this cause.

She turned and those big eyes of hers pulled at his heart. "There you go. I can see the wheels turning in your head but you're not sharing it. Well, if you're hunting for a nice way to tell me that this all sounds preachy and not for you, I understand. People have passions for different causes. I wanted you to see the panther because we'll be releasing him soon and you said you want to feel something. This is where I find my joy. I don't know if it could be where you find yours, but if you think it could be, I'd like to share it with you."

It was hard to breathe. Despite the fact that they'd had sex, she wasn't pushing him to commit to her. A certain amount of insecurity would have been justifiable considering she'd been a virgin, but she wasn't making this about her. She was reaching out to him in the same spirit that she helped the animals at the rescue. He had a feeling that if he told her he couldn't stay, she wouldn't fight him, not because she didn't care, but because she cared unselfishly. "How long until the panther is released?"

"My mother said a little more than a week."

"You're okay with me staying here that long?" She took a moment to answer and Andrew's stomach tied up in knots. She chided him for keeping his thoughts to himself, but she was just as hard to read when it came to communicating what she wanted. He was beginning to see that she was extremely empathetic both with animals and with people and tended to put the needs of others before her own. He didn't want that to be the case with him.

Finally, she nodded. "I think it would be good for you."

He lost his patience then and backed her up against one of the trees. "And what about you?" He cupped her face with one hand while placing his other possessively on her hip. "What do you want?"

Her pupils dilated and her breathing became audible. "I

told you, I'm okay with you being here."

"That wasn't what I asked you," he growled and kissed his way up her cheek to her ear. "Forget about what you think you should say." He nipped at her earlobe. "I know what I want." He trailed kisses down her neck to her exposed collarbone then raised his head and looked down into her eyes, loving how flushed and excited she looked. "You. Again and again until we both forget about everything else. Is that what you want?"

Her chest was heaving against his and her breath was a hot caress across his lips as his mouth hovered over hers. "Yes."

Her softly uttered agreement was enough for him to give in to his hunger for her. Their kiss was hot and intense. She squirmed against him, exciting him more. He forced himself to take it slowly, savoring every flick of her tongue against his, every sound she made, as his hands moved over her. Although he wanted to rip her shirt off her, he didn't. A small corner of his brain had the sense to remember the cameras her parents had mentioned. Now that he was sure they wanted the same thing, it didn't have to happen there. He raised his head, caught his breath and rested his forehead against hers. "How far away is that hotel your parents mentioned?"

Confusion entered her eyes. "You don't want to stay here anymore?"

He ran a thumb over her parted lips. "We can sleep here, but what I want to do to you shouldn't happen where your parents can hear you crying out for more. There's no reason we can't say we have errands to run, is there?"

Her tongue darted out to circle the end of his thumb. "I'd like that."

"Lenny? Andrew? Dinner is ready," Art's voice called through the woods.

Andrew exchanged a look with Helene and they both burst out laughing. She said, "I hope this isn't one of the places they set up cameras."

He gave her a quick kiss. "Do your parents usually call you in for dinner?"

Her cheeks went bright pink. "No." She called back to her father, "We'll be right there."

They both laughed again and separated. He took her hand and laced his fingers between hers. "Then I'm sure they won't even ask where we're going when we say we need to go into town."

They shared another laugh as they headed back. As they approached the spot where the path widened, Andrew stopped and brought Helene to a halt beside him. There was something he wanted to say before they were with her parents again. "Helene?"

"Yes?"

"What you do here is remarkable. Thank you for sharing it with me."

The gentle smile she gave him shot right through the walls he'd built around his heart and shook him to the core. As if she knew he needed a little comic relief, she joked, "We'll see if you're singing the same tune tomorrow after you clean out a few pens."

He chuckled, knowing he would be. Manual labor had never scared him. As Emmitt had reminded him, his head was in a better place when he kept his body busy. There was lightness in his step as they started walking again. For the first time in a very long time, he was where he wanted to be.

Chapter Thirteen

T EN DAYS LATER, Helene was driving back after meeting with a concerned gas station owner who had expressed a fear that having a panther in his area would put his employees in danger. He'd become more and more vocal as the date of the panther's release neared. Armed with maps, data, and the phone numbers of people who had accepted panthers into their area without incident, she'd spent over an hour reassuring him. Although he couldn't legally block the release of the panther, nervous people called animal control over every rustle in the bushes until an animal was considered a nuisance even if it wasn't. What seemed to win him over in the end was the tag that made it possible to always know the location of the panther.

It had been an emotional meeting, and Helene was glad Andrew hadn't attended with her. The man had yelled at her to get a few of his early points across. Helene was used to working through such conversations, but Andrew might have felt he needed to protect her. Thankfully the panther's final veterinarian visit was that morning, and Helene's father had requested Andrew's assistance. If all went well, the still tranquilized panther would be loaded into his travel crate for his trip to freedom.

Andrew had originally said he would stay to witness that. Helene didn't know if that meant he had plans to leave after the release. It was a topic they'd avoided since that first day at the rescue.

There were a growing number of those—topics they pretended were non-issues. Although they'd spent every day together and slipped away each evening for a blissful romp at a hotel, Andrew had kept parts of himself closed to her. He wouldn't talk about his family. He avoided any mention of his time in the Marines. Without discussing it, they'd come to a mutual agreement to not talk about what had happened in Aruba.

It was impossible to be upset with Andrew for what he withheld because he was so wonderful in other ways. He not only helped out at the rescue, he also seemed to genuinely enjoy her parents, and they liked him. He'd encouraged Helene to join him each morning for a run, a feat that had been hellish for her at first, but was getting easier. She didn't have his stamina, but when she needed to walk, he walked beside her. He'd ask her a question and listen as if the sound of her voice was a pleasure to him.

On the outside they looked like any other couple, but Helene knew they couldn't go on this way indefinitely. She was unable to talk with anyone about her gnawing sadness over her uncle. Andrew had found a place where he could escape whatever haunted him, but avoidance wasn't the same as healing. The pain she'd witnessed in Aruba was there, locked within him, and it was only a matter of time before something would make him face it again. Would he find another place to hide when that happened?

We're lovers. I'd like to think we've become friends. Are we more? Is more even possible for two people who met the way we did?

Helene pulled onto the dirt road that led to the gate of the rescue. A convertible Maserati was stopped in front of the gate. The driver was in a charcoal suit, and his hand was hovering over the keypad. It wasn't unusual for someone Helene didn't know to come to the rescue, but when the man swung around to look at her it was obvious he wasn't happy. He turned the engine of his car off and got out, slamming the door of the convertible.

Who was he? And what was he doing there? There was only one way to find out. Helene stepped out of her vehicle.

He strode toward her and the dark expression on his face brought back how Helene had felt in Aruba when she'd realized her uncle was afraid enough to desert her. *Fear.* She took a step back and rethought the wisdom of facing him on her own. He wasn't one of the people after her uncle, was he? "Who are you?" she called out.

"Who are *you*?" he snapped back.

Helene had never been the type to turn and run, but she'd left her cell phone in the car and was quickly realizing how foolish that might have been. She decided she didn't care what he thought of her, before she gave into the panic that was nipping at her, she needed to ask her father if he was expecting anyone.

She bolted back into her car, closed and locked the door. Frantically, she searched through her purse for her phone and dialed her father's number. No answer.

The man was already at her car window. He knocked on it and told her to lower it. She shook her head and waved her phone at him. He threw his hands, yelled something to her, then strode back to his car. Ring. Ring. Ring. No answer.

The man reached inside his car for something and was turning around with it in his hand when bullets rained down in a straight line between the cars. Helene screamed. The man spun, ducked down, and ran to the passenger side of her car. He was yelling again and trying to open it.

Okay, this shit is real. Her parents and Andrew were inside the rescue. She dialed Andrew. Everything she'd held in, every fear she'd pushed aside, came rushing in until she couldn't think. As soon as he answered, she cried out, "They're here. They found us. Please keep my parents safe. Promise me you won't let anything happen to them."

ANDREW HAD BEEN smiling when he'd answered his phone. His time with Helene and her family had filled him with a sense of peace he hadn't thought he'd ever find again. Like her, they didn't require him to be perfect. He was beginning to feel that he'd finally found where he belonged. He'd not only found a woman he couldn't get enough of and a cause that needed him, but, in a similar way to how she felt, the rescue made sense to him.

I fit here.

A few minutes earlier her father had been lamenting

about how he hated shooting tranquilizer darts when the animal was as far away as the panther was. Andrew had held out a hand, her father had handed the rifle over, and Andrew had made the shot easily. The proud look in Art's eyes was what Andrew had always missed with his own father.

Then he heard the panic in Helene's voice and instantly transformed to Marine mode. He barked for Art and the veterinarian to go back to the house and get Rose inside as well. "Get back to the main house."

"What the hell is going on?" Art demanded.

"I don't know yet," Andrew said, then turned his attention back to Helene. "Where are you? What do you mean they found us?"

"I'm at the gate. Someone is shooting at me from the trees. There's a man trying to get into my car. This has to be the people my uncle was afraid of. Who else could it be? Oh, my God. I don't know what to do."

"Get out of there," Andrew commanded.

"I can't. I can't leave. Should I ram his car? What do I do?"

Andrew turned to Dr. Robbins. "Give me the keys to your truck." When the man hesitated, Andrew barked, "Now." As soon as he had the keys, he said, "I'm coming. If someone is shooting from the trees and not hitting anyone, that's my men, and those were warning shots. Who's at your car?"

"Your men?" Art asked, grabbing Andrew's arm to halt him.

"I don't know. I don't know who he is, but he's not

happy." Then Helene asked in a panic at the same time, "What do you mean your men?"

"I told you I'd keep you safe," Andrew said to Helene. To Art, he said, "I'll explain later."

"No way. I'm coming with you," Art said. "What kind of trouble have you brought to my family?"

There wasn't time to argue. Andrew jumped in the driver's seat while Art took the passenger side. They started off across the rescue, kicking up dirt as they flew down the unpaved roads.

"He's telling me to open the door. He says he'll get me out of here. Hurry, Andrew."

Andrew was using both of his hands to drive, and Art heard his daughter's fear.

"What are you two involved in?" he demanded.

"Later," Andrew said and threw the phone to Art. "Right now, we need to make sure this isn't who she thinks it is. Ask her to put her phone on video."

Art caught the phone even though he was being thrown around while Andrew took tight turns. "Honey, we'll be there in one minute. Hang on. Can you switch to video?"

"I'll try," Helene said in a rush. "I'm so sorry, Dad. I shouldn't have come home."

A moment later Art held up the phone for Andrew to see. Andrew slammed on the brakes, and quickly grabbed his phone back. "Shit. Helene, you're safe, but I have to call off my men." He sent a quick text to his team to stand down and fall back.

"What the hell is going on?" Art growled.

Andrew let his next words to Helene also be his answer to Art. "Helene, you're safe, do you hear me? That's Dax Marshall, my brother-in-law. Kenzi's going to kill me. My men just shot at her husband. Stay there. We're coming."

Chapter Fourteen

ANDREW HAD PEOPLE up in the trees? People with guns? And the furious-looking man banging on her window was his brother-in-law? She unlocked the car doors and the suited man jumped in the passenger seat.

"Are you hurt?" He scanned her as if expecting to see blood.

"No," she said, her mouth almost too dry to speak. "They were just warning shots."

"We need to get out of here. Do you want me to drive? You don't look so good."

Helene bet she didn't; her hands were shaking so much she'd dropped the phone onto the floor of her car, and she felt like she was about to throw up. "Andrew's calling off his men. We're safe. I think."

"Andrew's men? What the hell is going on here?"

Before Helene had time to answer, the gate of the rescue opened and a truck sped through it, coming to a dusty stop beside her car. Both her father and Andrew came running to her side of the car.

Her door was pulled open and Helene attempted to step

out, not sure her legs would hold her. She looked up at the trees, half expecting more gunfire. Not because she didn't trust Andrew, but because she once again felt like she was in a nightmare, and nightmares didn't follow the rules of reality.

Andrew pulled her out and into his arms, but she didn't stay there long. Her father grabbed Andrew by the back of the neck and yanked him backward.

Helene thought she knew what her father looked like when he was angry. She'd seen him go toe to toe, sometimes fist to fist, with some nasty people in the past, but she'd never seen him look as close to real violence as he did in that moment. He shoved her behind him and said, "No. You don't go anywhere near my daughter." He looked up from the man in the suit who was walking toward them to the trees and back at Andrew. "I let you in my house. Trusted you with my baby."

"Dad," Helene stepped out from behind him. "Andrew—"

"What have you gotten yourself mixed up in, Andrew?" the man Andrew had called Dax demanded.

"Who are *you*?" Art yelled at Dax.

"Family," Dax yelled back with more than a little impatience in his voice. "Who are you?"

Helene went to stand with Andrew. "Dad, Andrew is only trying to keep us safe."

"Safe from what?" her father barked into Andrew's face.

Instead of answering, Andrew put an arm around Helene and pulled her closer. He buried his face in her hair. "I will hire a hundred men to guard you every day for the rest of your life if it means never feeling like this again. All I could think was what if I didn't get to you in time."

Dax growled. "I came to check on you, Andrew, to make sure you're okay. I'm glad I didn't bring Kenzi with me. This is as far from okay as I've ever seen anyone."

"Will someone tell me what's going on?" her father demanded and Andrew raised his head.

In a tight voice, he said, "Anyone we tell has a chance of finding themselves in the same danger."

"Tell what?" Dax asked.

Helene met Andrew's eyes. Always the hero, he'd take a beating if it meant keeping others safe, but that wasn't what she wanted and she no longer saw it as their best option. "We need to tell them. I mean, what if it had been *them* today? People are safer if they're prepared."

"And I'd like to not be fucking shot at again by snipers you apparently haven't bothered to show photos of your family to," Dax said harshly.

Art was looking at Andrew in disgust. "My daughter never got so much as a speeding ticket. What did you drag her into?"

Helene stepped out of Andrew's arms, but took his hand in hers. "He didn't drag me into anything. It's not his fault. It's mine."

Her father shook his head, clearly not believing her.

"No," Andrew said, "it's not, Helene. Your uncle did this. It's all on him."

Maybe, but a part of her wished she'd never gone to

Aruba. "Dad, Uncle Clarence isn't the man you and Mom thought he was. He isn't who I thought he was either. He did some very bad things and warned us not to tell anyone, but maybe the advice of a coward is advice that shouldn't be taken."

"Who the fuck is *Uncle Clarence*?" Dax asked.

Art turned toward him. "I'd appreciate it if you don't swear in front of my daughter."

Dax threw his hands up again. "Yes, I can see that's what we should be concerned about right now."

Andrew snapped, "Go back to Boston, Dax. I didn't ask you to come here."

"That's it," Art said in a stern, authoritative voice. "Andrew, get in the truck. We're returning it to Dr. Robbins. If we're lucky, he hasn't already called the sheriff. We'll tell him whatever we have to, to get him out of here. He has a panther to release so he might swallow whatever we tell him. As soon as he's gone I want everyone back in the main house. No one goes anywhere before we talk this out. Are we clear?"

Helene had no idea what kind of reaction to expect from Andrew, but he held her father's eyes and nodded. "Yes, sir."

Art turned to Dax. "You and your fancy car can follow Helene to the main house, but don't go in."

Dax nodded his head once.

Art stood there, still tense and looking ready to punch someone. Helene let go of Andrew's hand and wrapped her arms around his waist. "I'm so sorry, Dad. I should have told you everything."

He hugged her to him. "Whatever it is, we'll figure it

out, Lenny. I just had my whole life flash before my eyes. Your mom and I pushed you out into the world, and if that had taken you away from us, I would have never been able to forgive myself."

If squeezing harder could have erased the last few minutes, Helene would have kept hugging her father, but there were things they all needed to do. "I'm fine, Dad. I'll meet you back at the house."

Her father took the keys from Andrew and took the driver's seat of the truck. He gave Dax a long look as if he considered demanding that he come along with them, but maintained his original plan.

Helene got back into her car and Dax walked slowly back to his. He pulled off to one side and let Helene take the lead. All three vehicles drove through the gate. The truck with her father and Andrew kept going, but Helene stopped in front of the house and Dax parked his car beside hers.

Her mother was beside the car, waiting for her as she stepped out. "You scared Dr. Robbins half to death. I convinced him to give you all a minute to sort things out." Her eyes went to the tall, suited man getting out of the Maserati. "What was happening out there and who's that?"

"Dax something, Andrew's brother-in-law."

"That's what this was all about? We had a visitor at the front gate? The way Andrew and your father peeled past the house I thought there'd been a crash or something."

Dax walked up and put out his hand. "Dax Marshall."

Her mother shook it. "Rose Franklin. It's nice to meet a member of Andrew's family. He's a tough one to get to speak about much."

Dax nodded. "Sounds accurate."

Her mother waved toward the house. "I guess this changes your plans to go along for the release?"

"Oh, yes," Helene said, still shaking on the inside.

"Well, let's go in where it's cooler. Would either of you like a glass of water or lemonade?"

Neither Dax nor Helene budged. Helene said, "Dad asked us to wait outside."

"Did he?" her mother asked, cocking her head to one side. "How odd. He must have thought I wouldn't be here, not that that would matter. Come on."

Dax folded his arms across his chest and sat back against the front of Helene's car. "I'll wait here."

Helene joined him. "Me, too."

"Is something going on?"

"Dad said we'll talk as soon as he gets back. If it's okay, Mom, I'd really rather only explain everything once."

Her mother gave her a long look. "You look a little wrecked. I'll bring drinks out here."

Helene and Dax thanked her.

After her mother had gone into the house, Dax said dryly, "I almost called ahead to tell Andrew I was coming but decided to surprise him."

Helene smiled slightly and met his eyes. He wasn't at all the scary character she'd imagined him to be. She quipped, "Hindsight." An awkward few moments passed, and Helene felt she had to say something. "So you're Andrew's family." Dax arched an eyebrow at her, and she forced a pained smile.

"And you are—?"

Helene looked away without answering. No matter how one wanted to live happily in denial, reality had a way of forcing its way to the forefront. Why would he want to tell his family about her? How could Andrew possibly explain her or how they'd met without lying? How could she ever look them in the eye and not feel awful for whatever role her uncle might have played in the death of one of their own?

Dax cleared his throat. "I'm here because my wife loves her brother, and she's worried about him."

Since he didn't know about Aruba, Helene had to ask, "Worried? Why?"

"He told her he would finish a tour in Iraq then head home in time for the holidays before going back. He didn't come home. He didn't reenlist. And no one knows why." Dax punched his leg. "Do you?"

Helene looked in the direction where she knew Andrew and her father were, even though she couldn't see them through the heavily wooded area. "I don't know the details, but even if I did, it would be something I'd leave for Andrew to share . . . if he's able to."

"What did he mean that people would be in danger if they knew about your uncle?"

Helene was saved from answering by the arrival of her mother with two glasses of water. Even though they'd met under crazy circumstances, she trusted Andrew. Again and again he'd proven to her that she could. All she had to do was stall until he came back and the two of them would figure out what to say together.

As soon as the truck started moving, Art growled, "You're going to tell me what's going on. I want to hear it now before you and my daughter have a chance to come up with a story you think will appease me."

"It's exactly as Helene said—Clarence Stiles got himself involved with some dangerous people. He asked me to bring your daughter home while he fled Aruba. He warned both of us not to tell anyone. Without saying why it was necessary, I couldn't tell you I'd hired men to watch the perimeter of your property—"

"Couldn't tell me? You've been with us well over a week. You're expecting me to believe that never in that time did your brain engage and think I might need to know any of this?" Art parked the truck back near the panther enclosure but didn't make a move to get out. "I let you into my house. I trusted you with my daughter. I won't make that mistake again."

Art threw the door open and got out. Andrew took a deep breath and did the same. He held his silence while Art clapped the vet on the shoulder and made light of the whole incident. "Stupid interns. Helene's been gone long enough to forget not to take their pranks seriously. This one just shaved five years off my life."

Andrew half listened to the story Art told the veterinarian, but all he cared about was getting back to Helene. Was she still scared? His men had texted that they'd fired because the man had looked like he was retrieving what might have been a weapon from his vehicle. Dax fit what Andrew had told them to watch out for: someone who would come in confidently and look as if he didn't belong. Hitmen weren't timid. He couldn't fault his men for reading the situation as they had, but he'd talk to them about their delivery.

Although, had there been an actual threat to Helene, their method might have saved her life. He shuddered, fighting back the horrific images that had filled his mind when he'd thought she was in danger.

On autopilot, he helped Dr. Robbins and Art load the panther into a travel crate. Dr. Robbins asked if he wanted to accompany him for the release and Andrew shook his head. He'd been looking forward to that ever since he'd first heard about it, but all he wanted at that moment was to have Helene back in his arms and assure her that he'd find a way to fix this.

A few minutes after the vet drove off Andrew and Art stood facing each other. Art said, "I want you and your men gone. I don't care what you have to tell Helene."

Andrew pocketed his hands and rocked back onto his heels. "I'll leave, but I will have people watching out for Helene. You don't know what you're facing. She needs the protection."

Art stepped closer, grabbing the front of Andrew's shirt. "Why? You say keeping me in the dark will protect me. I don't give a shit about me. My wife and my daughter are my life."

Andrew could have pushed Art away, but he didn't. He understood Art's desperation, and it moved him. This was Helene's father, though. What if telling him inspired Art to do something stupid that got him killed? What if her father slipped up and told someone or asked a question to the wrong person? Was it worth the risk? Andrew wasn't sure. He was willing to step in front of a bullet for Helene, but could he allow her father to do the same?

Art shook Andrew. "You bastard, who do I need to protect my family from?"

"I don't know," Andrew said and looked him in the eye. "If I did, they wouldn't still be breathing."

Art dropped his hand and brought it to his mouth. "For God's sake, help me protect my family. What happened in Aruba?"

Andrew took a long, calming breath. Helene might hate him for what he was about to do, but her safety was what mattered most to him. "My family sent me to Aruba to ask about something that happened a long time ago." As Andrew retold the events, he left out how he'd watched Helene before ever speaking to her. The date she'd gone on with the doctor was irrelevant as was the fact that he'd been unable to think of anything else but her since the first time he'd seen her. He did, however, retell precisely what Stiles had said regarding his involvement in the death of Kent. By the time he described how Stiles had burned his house to destroy the records before fleeing into hiding, Art was shaking his head as if it were all too much to absorb.

They stood there for a few minutes after Andrew finished.

"You brought her home after you learned what Clarence had done to your family?"

"She had nothing to do with that."

Art rubbed a hand across his forehead then he pinned Andrew with an intense look. "Tell me, would you trust your daughter with a man like you?"

Andrew chose brutal honesty. "With the man I used to be, yes."

Art studied Andrew's expression. "You've got ugly demons haunting you, don't you, son?"

"Yes, sir, and some days it feels like they're winning."

After a moment, Art asked, "Who do you have protecting my land?"

"The best retired Marine scout snipers I served with, men who taught me everything I know. I'll introduce you to them."

Art rolled his eyes heavenward. "Yes. I suppose I should meet them." He rubbed his forehead again. "I can't decide if you're a hero or a danger to everyone you're around. Do I call the law and have you hauled away or thank you for bringing Lenny home to us?"

Andrew didn't have an answer to that, so he said nothing.

Art turned and started walking. "Come on, everyone should be waiting for us back at the house."

Andrew wordlessly fell into step beside him.

After a few minutes of walking together, Art asked, "Will you tell your brother-in-law why there were people shooting at him?"

"Not if I can help it. No matter what role Stiles played in Kent's death, it won't bring him back. My mother mourned his death for a long time, and it nearly destroyed her. What would be the purpose of opening all that up for her again?"

They didn't speak again until they were near the house. "What if Helene already told him?"

Andrew shrugged. He'd thought of that, but Helene was surprisingly good at keeping her head in situations that would break most people. She wouldn't say anything unless she felt she had to. Either way, there was nothing he could do about it now.

If Dax does know, I'll convince him that no one else needs to. Like the rest of what was fucked up about his life, he'd contain the fallout.

When he saw Helene he fought the urge to run to her and pull her into his arms again. He wanted to hug her, reassure her, kiss her until she understood exactly how much she'd come to mean to him. He didn't, though. Instead, he kept pace with her father until they were standing just a few feet from where Helene was with her mother and Dax.

His eyes met hers. There was so much he wanted to say, but he didn't know where to even start. Did he start by apologizing for not telling her about the men he'd hired? Did he take her aside and break it to her that he'd told her father everything?

For a man who had spent his life making and standing by split-second decisions, he found himself strangled with uncertainty again. This was the damage he'd incurred in Iraq. It didn't show like a missing limb or a jagged scar. It couldn't be measured or eased with a painkiller.

He'd lost all faith in himself and his ability to be there for anyone else. Helene might end up being a hell of a lot safer with her father watching over her.

She was the purest, most caring person he'd ever come across. She deserved someone who could describe himself the same way. He didn't want her to be with him because she saw him as another creature who needed rescuing. He wanted to be the man she deserved.

She walked over to him and placed her hand in his. The simplicity of the gesture knocked the wind out of him. He turned and met her father's eyes. *I'll do whatever is best for Helene and for her family.*

God only knows what the hell that will be.

Chapter Fifteen

ALTHOUGH SHE DIDN'T know what had been said, Helene knew her father well enough to know he hadn't wanted time alone with Andrew to compliment him. Her father's expression was strained. Andrew looked disappointed. *Neither is bleeding. So, that's good.*

The presence of not only her mother, but also Dax, was enough to have the five of them staring at each other awkwardly. Her mother looked at each of them. "Did I miss something?"

Her father gave her a kiss on the cheek. "One panther is happily on his way to his new territory, Andrew shot his first tranquilizer rifle, and it seems that we have an unexpected guest. Isn't that enough?" He held his hand out to Dax. "The name's Art."

"Dax Marshall," Dax said, giving her father's hand a firm shake.

Helene was saddened by Andrew's reaction to his family. He'd told her he only went home when he had to, but seeing their strained relationship up-close broke her heart. She squeezed Andrew's hand tighter and willed him to say something.

He nodded at Dax. "Sorry I was occupied when you arrived. People who call first tend to get a better reception."

Dax's eyes narrowed. "I'll remember that."

Her mother said, "Dax flew in just to see Andrew and meet us. Isn't that wonderful?"

"Wonderful," Andrew said tightly.

"Are you staying somewhere local?" her father asked.

"It wasn't my intention to," Dax said.

"So you're leaving tonight," Andrew said like he was issuing a command.

"Yes," Dax answered succinctly. "And you're coming with me."

Andrew's eyes shot up. "I don't think so."

"Could you excuse us for a moment?" Dax asked.

Her father put his arm around his wife's waist and started to guide her away. "Let's go inside and start dinner. Come on, Lenny."

Helene had never been one to defy her parents. In fact she couldn't remember the last time she'd refused them anything, but nothing could have pulled her from Andrew's side. "I'll join you in a few."

"Now," her father said sternly.

Squaring her shoulders, Helene respectively said, "No, Dad."

He frowned.

Andrew bent and said, "It's okay. Go with your father."

She raised her chin. "I'm where I want to be. You didn't leave me when you could have, and I'm not going anywhere unless you tell me you don't want me here."

"I'll never say that." He closed his eyes briefly then tucked her to his side.

Her father went inside with her mother even though he didn't look happy about it. Helene laid a hand on Andrew's tense chest. "You're not alone."

"No, he's not," Dax said in a harsh tone. "He has a whole family who is worried sick about him. A family he can't be bothered to take a call from or even answer a text message."

"Go back and tell Kenzi you couldn't find me. She'll still love you. You're all she talks about."

Dax stepped closer. "You self-absorbed bastard. I don't know what the hell happened to you, Andrew, but it's time to get your shit together and think about how your actions are affecting others."

"Affecting them? I hear they've never been happier."

"Your family may not believe in pushing anyone to do anything, but I was raised differently. I'll kick your ass all the way to Boston if that's what it takes."

"I'm not going back," Andrew said dismissively, not sounding at all worried by the threat.

Dax growled and between clenched teeth said, "Your sister cries at night because she worries about you. You are slowly breaking her heart, and I won't sit back and watch you do it. I'm going to help you, if for no other reason than Kenzi loves you. That doesn't mean, though, that I don't want to punch you in the face right now. Wake the fuck up." He glanced at Helene. "Sorry for the language, Helene."

"No problem," Helene said automatically. Andrew's heart was beating double time in his chest, and his muscles were pulsing with tension.

"Tell her I'm fine," Andrew said.

"Tell her yourself," Dax volleyed back. He held out his phone. "Call and tell her how fucking fantastic you're doing."

"I'm not where I was," Andrew said angrily, ignoring the phone, and Dax pocketed it.

Dax let out an angry breath. "Thank God for that. Come back with me, Andrew. We'll get you help."

Andrew rose to his full height. "I don't need help."

Helene said softly, "But you do need your family."

Andrew glared down at her. "They don't need me. Not like this. On a good day I was too much for them. Now? I wouldn't last more than five minutes with them."

"I totally get it," Dax said. "Your family is dysfunctional. Completely off its rocker. Nuts beyond what even I thought was possible—"

"*But?*" Helene prompted him.

"But they love you, Andrew. Don't go back because you think it'll make you feel better; your brothers can be real assholes. They're going to say stupid shit to you because they aren't living your life. They don't know what you've been through. None of us do. But that doesn't mean we don't care. Kenzi needs to know you're okay. She needs to see you, hug you. Give her that, then you can come back here and hide all you want."

Andrew was quiet for a long moment.

"I'll go with you," Helene said as she cupped one side of his face with a hand.

"I don't need—"

"If you say you don't need me I will kick you in the shin so hard you'll be on your knees, spitting out dirt."

A hint of smile lifted the corners of Andrew's mouth. "That sounds hard."

"Oh, it would be," she said in a light tone.

Andrew looked across at Dax and shrugged, "She looks sweet on the outside, doesn't she? It's all steel under there."

Dax shook his head, but his anger was dissipating. "Good. I'll tell my pilot to ready my plane. We can be in Boston in a couple hours."

Andrew met Helene's eyes. "You don't have to come, Helene. My family is just as crazy as he says they are."

"As long as they don't shoot at me," she said without missing a beat, then in response to the shock in both of the men's eyes, asked, "Too soon to joke about it?"

Andrew kissed the top her head. "Are you sure you want to do this?"

Dax said, "She'll fit in just fine."

Looking back at the house, Helene bit her lip then said, "Which one of us wants to tell my father?"

DESPITE THE FACT that Helene was seated at his side, Andrew found the flight to Boston much less enjoyable than the flight to Florida had been. Dax sat across from them, and he wasn't the easiest conversationalist, especially when one wasn't willing to discuss anything Dax wanted to discuss.

He'd asked what Andrew had discovered in Aruba. He'd asked for the reason Andrew felt he needed to protect Helene. Andrew responded each time with vague answers that weren't really answers at all. Helene followed his lead. Eventually Dax had stopped asking anything and took out his laptop to work.

"We're going to see your family," Helene said when she caught Andrew's eyes on her.

"Only because you scare me," he said to make her smile.

She did. "Funny. Real funny."

He laced his fingers with hers and studied her hand. She didn't have the perfectly manicured nails of the women who surrounded his family. She kept them short, neat. Practical. They were as beautiful to him as every other part of her was. From her desire to help those who were hurt to her quirky sense of humor. From her face, bare of makeup, and still more beautiful than any woman he'd ever known, to the tips of her tennis-shoed toes, she was perfect. After everything she'd been through, was it wrong to inflict his family upon her as well? "Are you sure you want to do this? There's still time to escape if you've changed your mind."

"Are you kidding? I'm looking forward to meeting your family." When he didn't instantly share her enthusiasm, she said, "Tell me about them. Just so I won't be so lost when I meet them. Who's the oldest?"

"Asher."

"What's he like?"

A picture of his eldest brother came to mind, and he made a face. "It's his way or no way. We'd fight about which direction the sun came up, and it wouldn't matter if we both said from the east, I would still be wrong. There is no reasoning with him. At least, that's how he always was. He's married with a son now. I hear he's mellowed."

"Who's next?"

"Grant. He was born with a calculator stuck up his ass."

"Well, that's a nice image," Helene said lightly, and Andrew remembered what Art had said to Dax about watching his language around Helene. Andrew would never have used profanity in front of his mother or sister, but he was comfortable with Helene. He could be himself with her. Still, he vowed to pay more attention to how he spoke in front of her.

"He's not as bad as Asher, but I can only talk about my stock portfolio for so long before I find myself telling off-color jokes just to shake him up."

Helene chuckled. "I can see you doing that."

"My father would always intervene. He wouldn't say he was disappointed in my behavior, but he has this way of letting everyone know when he's not happy."

"Like pass the salt when the salt is nowhere near you," Dax chimed in without looking up from his computer.

Andrew frowned. He'd almost forgotten Dax was there. "Yes, like that."

"I don't understand," Helene said.

Andrew hadn't seen his father use that particular technique in years, but apparently it was still in his repertoire. "It makes a person stop, look for the damn salt, forget whatever they were saying, then realize my father is staring at them, waiting for them to make a better choice."

"That's genius," Helene said. "I need to try that. So, who comes after Grant?"

"Ian. He followed in my father's footsteps and went into politics. Although last I heard he'd become an ambassador or some shit like that. I don't keep up with him."

"What is he like?"

"It depends if he's happy with you or not. He's a brilliant negotiator, but he's another one who can't be wrong."

"Who's next?"

"Lance." Andrew smiled. "He's an architect. Very successful. He just got married to a woman he's been in love with since we were kids. Pathetic and kind of sweet at the same time. Willa's a really nice woman. They're expecting twins. I'm happy for him . . . for them."

"My friend, Clay Landon, is engaged to her sister, Lexi," Dax interjected, still typing as he spoke.

"Really?" Andrew said, "Hope he can handle her. She was always a wild one."

Dax looked up and smiled. "They're perfect for each other."

Helene gave his hand a squeeze. Her eyes seemed to ask if he had history with Lexi.

He shook his head. *No. Never. Nothing besides a shared addiction to shocking his parents.*

Her smile widened. It always amazed him how well she could read him. "There's so many of them. I'll try to keep them straight in my head. So, after Lance there's just Kenzi."

"Yes," Andrew said abruptly.

"What is she like?" Helene asked.

All typing paused and Dax looked up from his computer.

Andrew pictured his sister. "She's stronger than she knows, and braver than anyone thought she had to be. Like me, she spent a good deal of time away from the family, but she found her voice with them, and I'm proud of her. She married a real ass, but I won't hold that against her."

Dax threw back his head and laughed. Helene joined in. The mood was suddenly less oppressive.

"And your mother? Did you say her name is Sophie? What is she like?"

Andrew sat back and looked at the ceiling of the plane. "Fragile. Sad. She's the biggest reason I haven't gone home. I don't want her to see me until I have my head on straight."

"Not as fragile as you think," Dax said.

The lull in their conversation was broken by the pilot announcing they were beginning their descent. Helene searched her pockets for her cell phone then nodded and tightened her seat belt. "I'll need a moment to call my parents when we land."

"You could call them now," Andrew said. "There's a phone onboard."

"Thank you, but I promised my father I'd call as soon as my feet touched the ground. I also promised I'd call when we arrived at your parents' house. With how worried my father looked when we left, I wouldn't be surprised if he asked to speak to one of them."

"Are you serious?" Andrew asked.

She shrugged. "He doesn't know you. My mother wasn't upset until she looked your family up on the Internet. I think she's afraid I'll see how the other half lives and won't want to go back, but I'm not a poodle. We were given one once from the family of an elderly woman who had spoiled it horribly. The woman's children didn't want the dog because it barked and nipped."

"Wait," Andrew said with a smile. "Let me guess, it got loose and one of the bobcats at the rescue ate it."

"No," she said as if she were surprised he'd think that. "We placed him with a single woman my mother knows. She loves him, but he still nips."

"Where are you going with this story?" Andrew asked with a chuckle.

She waved a hand around to reference the expensive plane. "This is all nice, but I like my life in Florida. If money equated to Nirvana, we wouldn't see the children of so many rich people in the news caught with drugs or appearing in sex tapes, would we? They're poodles. I'd rather be a panther, scars and all."

Dax closed his laptop and coughed back a laugh. "You just say whatever you're thinking, don't you?"

Helene looked confused by Dax's amusement and Andrew's hand clenched on his thigh. "Be careful, Dax."

Dax raised a hand. "It's an observation, not a judgment. I actually prefer people who speak their minds."

"Me, too," Andrew said firmly. He took Helene's hand in his. "Helene, no matter how my family behaves, don't worry that you have to be anyone but who you are."

Helene looked back and forth between them. "How your family behaves? I don't understand."

The plane bounced as it touched down.

Andrew raised her hand to his lips and kissed her fingers. "And we don't have to stay a moment longer than you're comfortable with."

"Okay, now you're making me nervous. How bad could they be?"

Chapter Sixteen

HELENE DIDN'T ASK the question a second time because the expression on the faces of both men had said enough. They both expected her to have an issue with his family. She didn't normally have a problem with anyone so she wasn't overly worried. In general, people had always liked her. Yes, dating had been tough when she'd spent most of her time working with and likely smelling like animals, but she'd never had a shortage of friends. Teachers had always liked her. She couldn't remember the last person she hadn't gotten along with, except maybe Dr. Gunder after he'd pompously announced while pawing her that veterinarians weren't real doctors.

Dax walked to the front of the plane. Andrew helped her up but didn't lean down to kiss her as she'd expected him to. She thought at first it was because Dax was still on the plane, but it was more than that. Andrew's expression was cold and carefully neutral.

She touched his forearm in a prompt for him to look at her. When their eyes met she understood. *He's not even with his family yet and he's already withdrawing. He's preparing for the worst, not just for me, but for himself as well.* She wanted to hug him and tell him that everything would be okay, but since she had no idea what they were walking into, she held her tongue. She squared her shoulders as an urge to protect *him* surged through her and prayed that encouraging him to go home had been the right choice.

Andrew guided her to the plane's door and down the steps. A black limo was parked on the tarmac. As they walked down the steps, a woman rushed up to Dax and threw her arms around him. *That must be Kenzi.* She was beautiful but not at all stuffy in the way Helene had begun to imagine his family would be. There was no denying that she had been born to wealth, but there was a genuineness to her that Helene was drawn to.

Andrew's hand tensed in hers. When they reached the tarmac, the woman flew over to them. "Andrew!" She didn't hesitate. She stepped forward, hugged him tightly, and buried her face in the front of his jacket. "You're here."

He let go of Helene's hand to return his sister's hug. His face was white and pinched. "It hasn't been that long, Kenzi."

Kenzi loosened her hold and gave him a flat smack on his chest. "Why wouldn't you answer my calls or texts?" She covered her mouth with a hand and tears filled her eyes. "I was so worried that something had happened to you."

Instead of answering her question, Andrew turned, placed his hand on the small of Helene's back, and urged her forward. "Kenzi, this is Helene Franklin."

Kenzi wiped at her eyes and looked Helene over. "Nice

to meet you, Helene."

"Nice to meet you, too," Helene said. She offered her hand for a shake and Kenzi took it, but the exchange was awkward.

Dax placed his arm around Kenzi's waist and nuzzled her neck. "Happy?"

She wagged a finger at him. "I would have gone with you had I known where you were going."

Dax kissed his wife's cheek, appearing more amused than concerned with his wife's reprimand.

Kenzi gave her husband an indulgent smile then hugged him again. "Thank you."

"You're welcome," he said and kissed her briefly on the lips.

Andrew nodded at the limo. "We're staying at a hotel, but we'd appreciate the ride."

Kenzi exchanged a look with Dax. "We have spare bedrooms at our place."

"You know me, I'd rather have my own space," Andrew said.

"If you're sure. We can drop you there after we go to Mom and Dad's."

"I'll take Helene to see them tomorrow."

Kenzi's expression turned pleading. "No. You have to go tonight. After Dax called me, I told everyone you were coming home. They're already at the house waiting for you. We thought we'd have dinner together. All of us."

"You should have asked, Kenzi. We're tired."

Kenzi's expression fell, and Helene felt sorry for her. Helene wanted to kick Andrew for not seeing how much it meant to his sister to have him back. Helene said, "I'm not tired." Andrew frowned down at her. She had grown so used to his eyes following her with approval, desire, or both, that she almost apologized for overstepping. Then she took another look at Kenzi's sad expression and reminded herself that the right thing to do was often not popular at first but that didn't make it less imperative to do. Andrew needed his family as much as his family seemed to need him. *Let him be annoyed. He'll get over it.* "I'm really looking forward to meeting your family *and* I'm starving. I don't mind going without you, Andrew, if you want to go to the hotel and rest."

Checkmate.

He made a sound deep in his chest and glared at her.

She flashed a bright smile at him. *This is for your own good.*

"I couldn't let you do that," he said tightly. "Dinner it is."

Kenzi studied them both for a moment, then pulled her coat tighter around her. "Great. Then let's get going."

Helene shivered in the light coat she'd grabbed from her house, but said, "I'll meet you in a second."

Kenzi hesitated, but Dax reassured her that everything was fine. Andrew looked as if he wanted to wait with her but she waved him to go with them. As soon as she was alone, she called her parents. "I'm here," she said.

After her parents spent a minute situating themselves so they could both hear her, her mother asked, "How was the flight?"

"Nice. It went by fast."

"And his family?" her father demanded.

"We just got here, so I can't say much, but his sister seems lovely. She was so happy to see him."

"Oh, that's great," her mother said.

"I only have a minute, but I wanted to say something."

"Okay," her parents said in unison.

"Thank you for understanding how important this is to me. I really want this to work out for Andrew."

"We know," her mother said gently.

"Don't see it as a failure on your part if it doesn't work out there. Not every family is like ours," her father added.

Love for her parents welled within her. "I'm realizing that, and it makes me even more grateful to have the two of you. I love you."

"We love you, too," her mother said.

"We sure do," her father chimed in.

"We're headed over to his parents' house for dinner. Looks like I'll be meeting the whole bunch of them tonight."

"Just be yourself," her father said.

"That's what Andrew said."

Her mother clicked her tongue. "My mother used to say, 'Give 'em your best and if that ain't good enough, give 'em hell.'"

Her father laughed, but said, "Grandma was senile at the end. You might want to go easy on following all of her advice. But don't worry, Andrew's family will love you."

"Are you staying with his parents?" her mother asked. "If

so, you might want to get a hotel room there, too. With all the 'errands' the two of you have, his parents will probably be more comfortable with you not doing that in their home."

Helene blushed to her toes. She hadn't realized her parents knew where she and Andrew had disappeared to each day. "Okay, well, good talk. I'll call you either tonight or tomorrow morning."

"Be good," her mother said.

"Be careful," her father added. "Love you."

"Love you, too." Helene hung up and rubbed her cold hands together. The driver of the limo opened the door as she approached it. Helene slid in and chose a spot next to Andrew.

"Everything okay?" Andrew asked. Although he seemed concerned, he didn't pull her to him as he normally would have. A search of his face revealed a lack of any emotion. This was what Helene had feared, he was shutting down.

He was a complicated man. Strong and guarded at times, tender and silly at others. When she'd gone to rush into her uncle's burning home, she'd seen the depth of his pain and scars. Visiting his family was revealing yet another side of him. He was withdrawing both emotionally and physically. What was he afraid would happen? He'd said he hadn't gone home mostly because of his mother. He didn't want to go home damaged. *Does he think what he's been through has made him unlovable? He's wrong.*

I'm falling hard and fast.

Is everything okay?

"Yes," she said. *I have to believe it is.*

HELENE'S REAPPEARANCE WAS a welcome reprieve from the conversation Andrew had been having with his sister. It had started the moment the door of the limo had closed, allowing Kenzi, Dax, and him a moment of privacy.

Kenzi had immediately said, "Are you and Helene serious? I've never heard you mention her name. How long have you known her?"

Andrew wasn't about to tell her any part of how he'd met Helene nor was he ready to define their relationship. "It's good to see you, too."

Dax had taken her hand in his. "Give him a moment to breathe, Kenzi."

"He's never brought anyone home before, Dax. My parents will be asking the same questions." Kenzi leaned forward. "While we have a minute, Lance heard you went to Aruba. Did you find out anything? I told him the private investigator is exaggerating everything just to milk him for more money. He called and told Lance the man who ran the clinic where I was born fled the country after his house burned to the ground. Do you know anything about that?"

The door of the limo had opened then, perfectly timed to make a response unnecessary. Now Helene was looking at him with her lips pressed together in determination. He guessed she was disappointed in him, but the lure of going into survival numbness was too strong. Kenzi said something to her that made Helene smile, but he'd missed what it was.

He yearned for the simplicity of being with Helene in

Florida. He wanted to wake up, work hard, laugh with people who didn't ask him questions he didn't have the answers to, and lose himself in mind-blowing sex with Helene. It took coming back to Boston to realize ten days in heaven hadn't cured him. The guilt and self-loathing were suffocating.

The ride to his parents' home passed in a blur. Before long, well before he was ready, the limo pulled into their driveway. The driver held the door while Helene and Dax got out. Kenzi hung behind. Andrew half stood to follow them out.

"Andrew," Kenzi said.

"Yes?"

"I love you. You don't have to tell me what happened to you. You don't have to tell anyone. I just want you to know I'm always here for you."

Andrew nodded and finished getting out of the vehicle, then held his hand out to her. "I know." She stepped off to join Dax, and he cursed himself for not saying he loved her, too. It wasn't her fault he was fucked up.

Helene was at his side, and he frowned at her. *Her first time meeting my parents shouldn't be like this. I should be laughing, and she should be dancing with excitement. I'm sorry, Helene. Sorry I can't do this better.*

Her eyebrows furrowed as if she was trying to read his thoughts. "Are you angry with me?"

"No." He shook his head. "Myself. I shouldn't have brought you here. You don't need this crap. What the hell are you doing with me?"

She caressed his cheek softly. "Falling in love for the first time in my life. So stop looking like this is the worst day of your life. We've got this." She dropped her hand and took a step toward the house. "Are you coming?"

He stood absolutely still, her words crashing over him like a tsunami overwhelming the shore. He'd retreated so far within himself that it took a minute or so to be sure he'd heard her right. "Don't," he said hoarsely. "Don't fall in love with me."

She pressed her lips together again and her unwavering eyes held him in their spell. "You can say you don't feel the same, but you can't tell me how to feel." She waved a hand over her face and chest. "Sweet on the outside. Steel underneath."

With a half smile, he pulled her into his arms. "I don't fucking deserve you."

She kissed him, and for a moment everything else dissolved away. When their kiss ended, she smiled up at him with tears in her eyes. "Yes, you do. Give me a chance and I'll prove it to you."

Her claim reminded him of how she'd sounded when she'd defended her uncle. Andrew shuddered against her. He'd once been fearless in the face of the unknown. Danger was a challenge he'd run toward, until he'd seen too many men die that way. He'd thought age and experience had tempered that cockiness until he'd packed Lofton into a body bag. As close, if not closer, than Andrew was to any of his biological brothers, Lofton had been his family. *I failed him. Failed his wife. His daughter.*

God, I miss him.

Part of him wanted to drive Helene away before he failed her, too.

Part of him wanted to hold her until her faith in him led him back to himself.

He could have said the words she was probably hoping to hear, but he wasn't ready to. He just stood there, holding her.

"Come on in, Andrew. Everyone is excited to meet your friend," his father's voice called out from the steps.

Andrew didn't look away from Helene. "Thank you for coming here with me."

She smiled. "It'll be good. You'll see."

Andrew stepped back and took her hand, leading her up the stairs to where Dale Barrington was waiting. "Dad, this is Helene Franklin."

His father smiled cautiously. "Nice to meet you, Helene."

"You, too." Helene pounced on his father and gave him a tight hug that took him completely by surprise then looked back at Andrew and winked.

Andrew almost smiled as he stepped forward. He and his father had often found themselves on opposite sides, especially since Dale's top priority had been to keep family events peaceful. If he knew the baggage Andrew was carrying this time, he likely wouldn't let him in the door.

Andrew shook his father's hand. "Dad."

"Andrew. It's good to see you."

"You, too."

"Come in. Come in. Your mother hasn't been able to sit since she heard you were coming."

The door behind his father opened and his mother appeared as if on cue. "Andrew!"

Andrew walked into her arms. She pulled back and took his face between her hands. "How are you?"

"Fine," he answered automatically. Throughout his life it had been the only allowed response. Everything went smoother if he kept his reactions contained to what his parents expected.

His mother studied his face, looked as if she wanted to ask him a question, but didn't. Instead she looked past him and smiled. "You must be Helene. Kenzi was telling me about you."

"All good," Helene joked and hugged his mother in greeting.

"Of course," his mother said graciously and linked her arm with Helene's. "Everyone is waiting to meet you."

When they were out of earshot, his father said, "You had us pretty worried."

"I don't want to argue, Dad," was all Andrew said before following Helene and his mother into the house.

His father sighed audibly and closed the door behind him.

As soon as he entered the foyer, his brothers headed for him like warships cutting through choppy water. He looked around. Helene was already in a circle of his sisters-in-law, holding a baby. Seeing her with them twisted his gut painfully. Could he ever give her that?

"Nice of you to finally show your face," Asher said in his usual tone.

"Take it easy, Asher. He doesn't even have his coat off yet," Ian advised smoothly.

Asher looked him over. "From the stories I heard, I expected you to look like shit."

Grant appeared at one side of Andrew, Lance on the other.

Sporting a tight smile, Andrew said, "Funny how no one gets it right. People told me you were easier to get along with now that you're a father."

"Always a joker," Asher said harshly, "but there's nothing funny about what you put the family through. You couldn't answer one call? Text Mom that you weren't dead?"

Andrew would have said something, but he looked up and saw his mother watching them. He'd come home to make them feel better, not worse. "I'm here now."

Ian said, "Is it true that you're not a Marine anymore?"

The youngest of his brothers said, "I believe they say, 'Once a Marine, always a Marine.'"

"Whatever," Ian said. "You didn't reenlist after your last tour?"

"Correct," Andrew answered shortly.

Grant put a hand on his shoulder. "What's your next step? If you want help planning it out, my door is always open. You've left your trust fund just sitting there. It would have a lot more in it if you did something with it."

Lance said, "Grant, he can talk about that anytime. I want to know about your trip to Aruba."

"What trip to Aruba?" Ian asked.

"I asked him to go there to check something out," Lance answered.

"You were on the fucking beach, and you couldn't be bothered to call us?" Asher snapped.

Fighting to maintain his cool beneath their sustained interrogation, Andrew raised both hands and walked away without saying another word. He glanced at the liquor cabinet and clenched his hands at his sides. *No. Been there. Done that. Don't need it.*

But I do need air. Without thought of how it would look to Helene or his parents, he whipped open the door and stepped back out into the cool evening. He inhaled deeply then tensed when he felt a hand on his shoulder.

From behind him, Asher growled, "I'm not done."

"I am," Andrew said, not turning back to face his brother. His anger with himself was rising and intensifying his irritation with Asher. "Don't touch me."

"What the hell is wrong with you?" Asher asked, dropping his hand.

"What's wrong with *you?*" Helene asked, and Andrew whipped around to see her plant herself between Asher and him. "This is your brother. You have to know him well enough to be able to see that he has been through a rough time. I convinced him to come here because I believed you love him. I don't know what usually happens here, but you need to back the fuck up. Instead of jumping all over him for not coming home, ask yourself why he didn't. It's glaringly obvious to me."

Andrew took hold of Helene's arm and tried to step in front of her. The last thing he wanted to do was have to kill Asher for unleashing his temper on her. She wouldn't budge, though, so he compromised and stood beside her.

Emily appeared at the door with her son on her hip. "Asher? What's going on?"

Asher threw his hands up in the air. "I'm talking to Andrew and his girlfriend."

Emily looked at each of them. "How's that going?"

Asher's shoulders slumped. "Like shit." He ran his hand through his hair.

Emily bounced her son and said softly, "Maybe I can help. Andrew, Asher has been worried sick about you. He hasn't slept well since you didn't come home for Thanksgiving."

Andrew wanted to withdraw. He didn't want to have this awkward conversation or open himself to the memories of why he hadn't come home. Helene's hand grasped his, though, and when he met her eyes the hope he saw there left him with little choice. "I don't want to talk about where I've been. I want to come in, visit with Mom and Dad, show everyone I'm fine, and fly out tonight."

A heavy silence hung over the four of them. Helene said, "In the wild, two adult alpha males naturally clash. They fight until one of them is driven off for good. Humans are supposedly more evolved. You don't have to lecture your brother, Asher. You don't have to be right this time. This time, just tell him you love him."

"Helene, stop," Andrew said.

"No," Helene turned to look at him. "What your brother just did was wrong, and he knows it."

The doorway behind Asher was filled with wide-eyed members of his family. Although the brothers argued often, no one called Asher out for his behavior, especially not at his parents' home. Helene, though, was a woman who feared nothing, not wild animals, nor raging brothers. His eyes flew to his mother's, worried that the scene might be too much for her, but she was handling it better than he would have thought.

Asher let out a long breath. "Don't leave, Andrew. Especially because of me." Emily went to stand beside him. She handed their son to him. Asher looked down at the smiling face of Joseph and then back at Andrew. "I'm only angry with you because I thought something had happened to you."

Andrew almost said, "Something did," but instead nodded once.

Asher turned his son against his shoulder. "Sorry." Emily elbowed him and gave him a pointed look. "I do love you. We all do."

His father cleared his throat. "Why don't we bring this all back inside and start over?"

One by one, his family turned and walked back in the house until only he and Helene remained on the steps. He bent and whispered against her lips. "Any minute you'll realize that being with me is not worth all the shit I've brought into your life."

She went on her tiptoes and between kisses said, "I'll

never say that."

A few minutes later, after sharing a deeply passionate kiss, they stood simply holding each other. "You deserve to be with someone who can love you."

Her eyes turned sad. "And that can't be you?"

He hugged her tighter. He wanted to say it could be, but the man he'd been wouldn't have walked out of the house and left her with his family. He wouldn't promise her anything until he knew he'd be there for her, not battling shame and confusion. He still felt nothing for himself beyond disgust. How could a man like that love anyone?

Chapter Seventeen

IN WHAT COULD only be described as a surreal turn of events, Helene found herself seated at a large table having dinner with Andrew's family as if nothing unusual had occurred. Conversation was polite. Stories were told and laughter occasionally erupted.

Helene remembered what Andrew had said about his mother being fragile and everyone tiptoeing around her. She wondered what his family thought of her. Not that fear of their opinion would have changed a single thing she'd said.

She cringed as she remembered her choice of words. She'd never been one to swear or to cause a scene, but something inside her had snapped when she'd watched Andrew's brothers essentially run him out of the house. She'd understood Andrew's withdrawal. From the way he'd described his family, there was no winning unless he chose to push back, and he didn't feel he could do that without upsetting his mother. She wasn't proud of how she'd handled the situation, but if she was allowed to do it all over again she wasn't sure she'd do it better. She'd been angry *for* Andrew. He needed his family's support, not to get into a shouting match with them. Andrew didn't want to give himself anything else to regret, and that's why he'd removed himself.

It was also why he was pushing her away.

She thought about what Andrew had said just before they'd come back into the house and a wave of sadness swept through her. He not only didn't love her, he didn't see it as a possibility in the future. It hurt to hear it. While conversation buzzed around her, she sat quietly, and the realization that he meant more to her than she meant to him sunk in. She excused herself and sought the solace of the guest bathroom.

After washing her hands a few times, she met her eyes in the mirror. She thought about something her father had said when he'd walked in and caught her crying over a raccoon they'd tried to save, but who had ultimately died of complications from internal injuries. She'd apologized and told him she was trying to not break down every time they lost an animal. He'd said, "There's no shame in crying, honey. You love animals. Love is what keeps us caring and no matter how things turn out, it's always worth the pain."

Always worth the pain.

She was definitely more carefree before she'd met Andrew, but she couldn't wish she hadn't met him. She'd meant it when she'd said she was falling in love with him. He'd brought a whole side of her to life, a side she hadn't known was dormant. If he hadn't come into her life she wouldn't know what she wanted from a relationship. He had deepened her understanding of what was possible and given her insight into even her own parents' marriage. They were partners both in marriage and in their passion for the rescue. Perhaps because they had experienced some intense situations, the bond between Andrew and her was strong. He might worry that he couldn't be there for her the way he thought he should be, but he'd already proven that he wouldn't leave her. With actions, if not in words, he'd already shown that her safety was his priority.

He's probably feeling guilty about walking out of his parents' house without me, but I get it. I pulled him into what he said he wasn't ready to face. If I had one do-over, I would let him come here on his terms.

She dabbed her tears away. *He needs me to be strong. I can cry later when this is all over.*

She stepped out of the bathroom and came to a skidding halt when Andrew's mother called out her name.

"I didn't mean to scare you," Sophie said, stepping close so she could lower her voice. "I wanted to thank you for bringing Andrew to us."

"You're welcome, but it was really Dax who brought him back," Helene said, clasping her hands before her.

Sophie reached out and laid a hand on Helene's. "I'm so glad my son found someone like you."

Helene's eyes filled with tears. She wanted to believe he felt that way. "He's an incredible man."

"Yes, he is. He's hurting, though, isn't he?"

Since it was far from a secret, Helene nodded.

"Has he told you why?"

Helene shook her head.

Sophie brought a hand up to rub her temple. "It's my fault, you know. I faced something ugly once, and I let it beat me. My husband worried about me so he kept our house peaceful. We didn't realize what message we were sending to our children. When things go wrong, they don't know how to turn to each other for help. They snap because they've never talked things out. Asher truly does love and admire Andrew, but none of my sons are comfortable talking about their feelings. He needed to hear he wasn't expressing himself appropriately. We're not perfect, but when it matters, we're there for each other. Especially since Kenzi opened my eyes to how my pain had affected the family. It wasn't easy to hear, but it brought us closer together. I'm not perfect and I don't need my children to be. I want to be there for them, for the good times and the bad times. I don't want to miss out on any more than I already have."

"Have you said any of this to Andrew?" Helene asked.

Sophie opened and closed her mouth for a moment then said, "No. Not yet."

"You should. He needs to hear it."

Sophie wiped a tear from the corner of her eye. "Before you leave, I'll take him aside and tell him."

"That'll be good for both of you, I think."

Sophie nodded. "Don't let this visit run you off. We're actually a very nice family once you get to know us. I hope you'll give us a chance and come back again."

Helene wanted to reassure Sophie, but knowing this visit might be her last made her choose her words carefully. "I'm sure I will. Sorry about how I acted earlier. That wasn't the best first impression of me."

Sophie studied her face quietly then said, "You were beautifully fierce for all the right reasons. Asher can still be a hammer at times when a softer approach would work better. With Emily he's a lamb, but he has always charged in first and reflected later. I wish I knew how to get those two boys to see that they are more alike than they are different. My greatest fear is my children end up like my sister and I did. We never did find our way back to each other. She was a stranger to me by the time she died, and I regret that as much as I regret anything else. That's not the lesson I wanted to pass on to my children. It would break my heart to see their relationships with each other become irreconcilable."

Helene wasn't sure what to say so she made sympathetic sounds and gave Sophie's arm a supportive rub. "I'm sure it won't come to that."

Sophie smiled sadly. "I'm so sorry to lay this on you. I spent so many years holding everything in that it bursts out of me at times."

"It's okay. I understand."

"Andrew said your family lives in Florida. Are you close?"

"Very, my mother is my best friend."

"What does she think of Andrew?"

"She says he's amazing."

"And your father?"

Helene smiled ruefully. "He was understandably concerned when he first heard I was coming here, but he trusts my judgment. I told him this was important, and he's being supportive of both Andrew and me."

"I'd love to meet them sometime," Sophie said.

Helene whipped out her phone. "Really? You have no idea how much better it would make them feel if you said a few words to them now."

"Oh. Now? Right now?"

"Sure." Helene dialed her parents' number. When her mother picked up, she said, "Mom. Dad. Put me on speakerphone. I'm here with Andrew's mother and she'd like to say hello."

Sophie accepted the phone and held it to her ear. She looked slightly uncertain when she greeted them. "Hello."

Helene watched and waited as her parents spoke. She could only see Sophie's expression and hear her side of the conversation, which made it tricky to gauge how it was going.

"Yes, Sophie Barrington. Helene and Andrew are at our home having dinner with my other children." There was another pause while Sophie listened, then she said, "Six. Five boys and one girl. Your daughter is absolutely lovely." Sophie's eyebrows arched. "No, I hadn't realized he'd been staying with you. An exotic animal rescue? How fabulous. I would love to talk more about what you do, as connecting good causes with donors is one of my passions." A moment or so passed as Sophie listened again. "Absolutely. Thank you for the invitation. Of course I'll speak to Andrew about it first. I don't want to intrude. The same for you. You're welcome to visit anytime. I'd love to show you Boston."

Sophie held out the phone to Helene. As soon as she had

it back, Helene held it to her ear. Her mother was already speaking.

". . . wonderful. Your father and I were sure things were fine, but we feel so much better now that we're sure. Now, go, have fun and don't give us another thought."

Her father said, "We don't care about the hour; call us tomorrow."

"I will," Helene promised. "Love you both."

"We love you, too." After pocketing her phone, Helene realized Sophie was still watching her. She reviewed what she'd just done and wondered if she'd made Sophie feel uncomfortable. "I'm sorry. I should have asked if you—"

Sophie cut off her apology by giving her a brief hug. She pulled back and blinked several times quickly. "I am truly blessed with the partners my children have chosen. You're exactly what my son needs. I hope he's in a place where he can see that."

ANDREW LEFT THE dinner table to check on Helene. He was cursing himself for bringing her into what had to be an uncomfortable situation. The drama that had initially erupted in response to his arrival had been replaced by forced, polite discourse that he found just as difficult to endure. He wanted to get out of there, and this time Helene was coming with him.

He hadn't realized his mother had also left the table until he saw her in the hallway having a conversation with Helene. *Oh, God.* He wasn't able to hear most of what they said, but he'd held back a laugh when Helene had handed her phone to his mother. He didn't need to ask to know who she had her talking to. His mother was far from shy, but it was fascinating to watch her interact with a whole different level of friendly. Helene didn't polish things up. Despite what they'd seen in Aruba, she had retained her confidence. There'd been no hesitation in handing the phone over to his mother, and he admired that about her. She was naturally optimistic without being unrealistic.

She was also thoughtful. She hadn't called her parents because they'd demanded that she do it. She hadn't put his mother on the phone because someone had pressured her to. She'd wanted to ease her parents' concerns. How they felt was important to her.

Just like she values how I feel. She's here because she cares about my relationship with my family.

Hearing his mother say, "I am truly blessed with the partners my children have chosen. You're exactly what my son needs. I hope he's in a place where he can see that," made it sound as if it were merely a matter of choosing Helene.

It wasn't that simple.

He stepped closer and said, "So this is where you both went."

Helene turned to face him with a start.

Sophie exchanged a look with her then said, "Do you have a moment, Andrew?"

"Of course," he said, but first went to hover over Helene. Her eyes were red and puffy. "Are you okay?"

Helene nodded. "Absolutely."

"I'll just be a minute then we can go if you want."

She gave him one of those long, heartfelt looks of hers that always left him feeling a bit shaken then smiled. "Take all the time you need. I hear the dessert is amazing."

He gave her a quick kiss on the cheek. "Save a piece for me."

"Save for you, eat for you . . . I'll decide when I see what it is." She winked.

He chuckled and she turned to make her way back into the dining room. Once he and his mother were alone, she touched his arm lightly. "Andrew, I'm so glad you're here."

"Me, too, Mom," he said.

"Don't lie. You're sorry you came home, but you shouldn't be. We needed to see you."

He hunched his shoulders. "I never meant to worry anyone. I know I should have—"

"Stop. You're here now, that's what matters." She touched his cheek gently.

"Is it?"

She searched his face again. "Andrew, I want to say something, and I'd like you to hear me out. Really hear me."

He shrugged, listening.

"When you were little, you brought every scrape or imagined boo boo to me because you knew I could make you feel better. When we lost Kent, I stepped away from that job without realizing it. I became so wrapped up in my pain and my guilt that I didn't see how my withdrawal hurt and affected all of you." Her voice broke. "It took an outburst from Kenzi to open my eyes."

"Don't get upset, Mom. That's the last thing I want."

She gripped his arm. "I don't want to fail you anymore. Any of you. I'm not made of fragile glass, Andrew. You can get angry with me. You can bring your problems to me. Families don't have to be perfect, and we're not. I know you're dealing with something. I can see it in your eyes. You don't have to tell me what it is, but you don't have to hide it from me, either."

For a moment he let himself believe in her and was simply a tormented man standing before his mother. He rubbed both of his hands over his face. "I fucked up, Mom."

She rubbed a hand over his back. "Oh, Andrew . . ."

He straightened. He couldn't do this. He couldn't put the weight of this on his mother. "I have to go."

She stepped in front of him. "You don't have to tell me what happened, but you can't keep it in, either. I did that, and it just got worse. Kenzi said she did the same and it tore her apart. Talk to someone, a professional or a friend. Don't keep this inside or it wins. The pain wins every time."

"I will." Andrew reached out and gave his mother a tight hug. She hugged him back just as fiercely. When he stepped back, his mother was still teary eyed but smiling.

She said, "When you have time, there's someone I'd like you to meet. Clay Landon is a friend of Dax's, and he started a foundation to help veterans."

Andrew sighed. "Thanks, but no thanks, Mom."

She nodded, but there was a silent determination about her, a strength of will that hadn't been there before. "So, I see you haven't given Helene a ring yet. How serious are you two?"

Andrew lifted and dropped a shoulder. "I care about her."

"She's good for you."

"Yes, but I'm not myself, Mom. Not yet. I don't know if I ever will be again."

His mother gave him a long, sad look. "She loves you."

"I know," he said in an equally sad tone and turned away. He didn't want Helene to love him. Not like this.

He returned to the dinner table, sat beside her, and took her hand in his. The love his mother had referenced was right there in her eyes when she looked at him, and it added another layer of guilt. It wasn't fair of him to continue as they were. She was offering her whole heart to a man who was only half there.

Chapter Eighteen

LATER THAT NIGHT, naked, Helene woke, still tucked against Andrew's chest. She smiled lazily as she remembered how their evening had ended with Andrew carrying her into their hotel room and making slow, tender love to her. There wasn't an inch of her he hadn't adored. It was confusing to feel sated even while so much was left unsaid. "Andrew?"

He kissed her forehead. "Yes?"

"Are you sorry we came to Boston?"

His chest rose and fell with the deep breath he took. "No. My family needed to see me."

His evasive answer didn't ease her confusion. How did he feel about seeing his family? Had it been too much? "I shouldn't have pushed you. I should have respected that you wanted to see them tomorrow."

"You meant well. I understand that."

Meant well? He wasn't giving her anything. "How did the talk with your mother go?"

"Good, I guess. She adores you."

Helene snuggled against his chest. "I'm easy to love."

He turned onto his side and ran his hand through her hair. "There's something I need to talk to you about."

The seriousness of his tone made her tense against him. Was it over? *Please don't let it be over.* "Yes?"

He sat up and turned on the light beside the bed. "What I'm about to tell you could ruin me if you ever made it public."

"I won't repeat it to anyone." She sat up also and clutched the blankets to her. The conversation wasn't the one she'd feared, but it looked just as painful for him.

"I don't know for certain that it was what my gut said it was, but I can't let it go."

"Okay." *Holy shit.*

"After everything we've been through, I feel like you might be the only one who could understand what I'm wrestling with."

"Say it. Whatever it is, just tell me." Helene slapped her hand down on the bed sheets between them.

THE LIGHT FROM the lamp didn't stop the memories from flooding in once he opened the door to the day he'd tried to forget so many times. He didn't start the story there, though. He started back when he'd met Dyonte Lofton during his first tour. They'd been paired to scout forward and an instant friendship had grown from discovering they could rely on each other. Lofton had become more of a brother to Andrew than any of his biological siblings had ever been.

He told Helene about the woman who had driven Lofton crazy during that tour, how he'd gone home to discover that she'd been sleeping with one of his friends for months, and how devastated he'd been. He retold how he'd teased Lofton mercilessly when his friend had first started talking to a woman, Gabrielle, who he'd met on a single's dating site. It had seemed like a sure-fire way to ensure history repeated itself.

Then Lofton came back after spending his leave with his online obsession and said he'd found his reason to keep fighting. No one had expected it to last. Deployments tested even the most solid of relationships, but his friend had found his mate and Gabrielle had accepted Andrew as if he'd been born his brother. He was best man in their wedding, Uncle Andrew to their daughter, and their home had always been open to him.

Andrew leaned his back against the headboard of the bed and closed his eyes. He described how excited he and the other three Marines had felt to be at the end of the tour. He explained that it was that excitement, that cockiness, that made not reviewing the details of the colonel's orders easy. The colonel had arranged every step of the mission, something Andrew normally would have done himself. He hadn't cared. In his mind, they were already on their way home.

When it came to describing what had happened, Andrew didn't pretty it up for Helene. He wanted her to know exactly what he was guilty of. He described how he'd been on the street watching for any trouble. Then the explosion. His friends inside. How deadly the rigged box had been when it had exploded. It had been instantaneous. He was back in that building, reliving carrying Lofton's bloodied, lifeless body to the Hummer. He struggled to breathe as he described the smoke that had choked his lungs as he'd run up the stairs to carry out the remains of another of his friends.

And then the contents of the box. The remains had appeared to be pieces of a Russian aircraft seat. How it hadn't made sense nor had it matched what the colonel had later said they'd been sent to retrieve. Lofton and the others had been given hero burials. Their families had received their Silver Stars for bravery. He'd received one as well, one that he'd put away in a drawer because he didn't feel he'd done anything to deserve it. No matter what his superiors told him, there'd been nothing heroic about leading his best friend and fellow Marines to their death.

Torn between the past and the present, Andrew met Helene's eyes and growled, "The contents of the crate were scattered around the room. I didn't see anything but pieces of a pilot seat. The colonel lied. We were there to pick up a personal trophy for his office. I have no proof, but I know it. What I don't know is if the truth is better than the lie he propagated. Gabrielle believes her husband was a hero. How do I look her daughter in the eye and tell her that her daddy wasn't a hero at all, he was just a casualty of a senseless illegal request that I would have refused if I had bothered to look into it? How do I tell them that he's gone because of me?"

Helene moved across the bed and wrapped her arms around him. She didn't say anything. She simply hugged him with her whole body.

"The guilt is slowly killing me, but is that any more than

I deserve? It would feel good to out the colonel, to bring him down, but that same victory would tear Lofton's family apart a second time. I used to know what to do, but I don't know this time."

They sat in silence for a long time. He had no idea what Helene thought, but she was the only person he trusted completely.

When she did speak it was in a tone he'd heard her use when she spoke about the importance of the rescue. "My mother says that inaction is humanity's greatest enemy. She says people don't wake up and decide to do nothing. Like you, when faced with two unacceptable choices it paralyzes them. What they fail to see is that it's not a matter of this or that. Solutions are rarely all one or all the other. Sometimes you have to fight part of the battle and count it as a win. If I were you, I'd ask myself if there was something I could do that might make things better without making them worse."

Andrew shifted so he was lying on his back again and pulled her down with him. He cupped her face with his hand. "That sounds like a bumper sticker—make things better without making them worse."

She shrugged and kissed his chest. "That's all I have. I would tell you that your friend's death wasn't your fault, that there was no reason for you to second guess your orders, but you know that." She tapped his temple softly. "Up here you know." She laid her hand over his heart. "This is where the problem is. Your friend wouldn't have wanted you to die with him. He wouldn't have wanted to leave you with the guilt, either. Maybe if you ask yourself what he would have wanted, maybe that's your answer."

He held her for a long time, long after she fell asleep in his arms. Her words echoed through him. What would Lofton have wanted?

Shortly after the sun came up, he slid out of bed, walked into the living room, and made several phone calls. When he was done, he wrote her a note and tucked it on the nightstand beside her. He bent and kissed her gently, careful not to rouse her, then he gathered his things and left the suite.

He finally knew what he needed to do. It was something he should have done months before.

Chapter Nineteen

ELENE KNEW SHE was alone before she opened her eyes. She touched her lips. Had he kissed her while she slept or had she imagined it? She told herself that he was most likely out for his morning run and that if she closed her eyes and didn't get up he'd be back when she woke again.

Her stomach churned when she saw a folded note on the nightstand. He might have written anything in it, but she *knew* it was goodbye.

She picked it up, lay back on the bed, and held it for a moment. *Whatever it says, I know what we have is real. It might have been too much for him, but that doesn't mean being with him was a mistake.*

She opened the note:

Helene,

I hired a car to pick you up and take you to the airport. Call the front desk when you're ready. There is a private plane waiting to take you home.

Thank you for last night and for every moment we've spent together. I'm sorry to leave you this way, but I know what I need to do now.

If I can, I'll come back to you, but I can't return until I know I can give you all that you give me.

Andrew

She hugged the note to her chest and closed her eyes. Halfway through the note, her throat had clenched because it had sounded like a man's last words, but the final sentence implied he'd chosen another course. She was relieved, but also sad he didn't feel she could be part of whatever he needed to do. Alone wasn't how her family handled their problems. She rolled over, picked up her phone, and called her parents.

She didn't tell them the details Andrew had shared with her. She would take those to her grave. She did, however, tell them he had shared painful memories with her, and then she read his note to them.

Ever the voice of reason, her father said, "You need to come home. He may be on his way to kill someone."

Her mother's lack of instant dismissal of that as unlikely was sobering. Helene took a moment to review everything she knew about him. From how he behaved when he was angry in Aruba to what he'd said he'd wanted for his friend's family. Killing the colonel would make things much, much worse without making anything better. "If he is, then I don't know him at all. Coming home now doesn't feel right. I'd feel like I left him."

"Honey, he left you," her mother said gently.

"No," Helene said firmly. Her uncle had left her. He'd

chosen his own welfare over hers. Andrew needed time, and she had to believe he was trying to find a way to heal, not only for himself, but for her. Whether he was putting himself in a mental health program or going back to see his friend's family, she needed him to know she believed in him. "He went to do something. He'll come back to me and when he does I want to be here in Boston with his family. They need me, too. They won't understand this."

Not missing a beat, her father asked, "Do you need us with you? We can be there by tonight."

A tear rolled down Helene's cheek as she considered how lucky she was to have the parents she did. She didn't need them holding her hand because their love was her strength. "No, I'm okay." She took a moment to fill her parents in on how dinner the night before had gone. She even told them what Sophie had said about how the death of her son had changed her.

Her father cleared his throat. "That couldn't have been easy for you to hear."

Her mother made a sad sound. "Your father told me about my brother and what happened in Aruba. I can't believe he had anything to do with that baby's death, but even if he did, you know that's not your guilt to carry, right?"

"I know," she said. She'd told herself that already, but it had taken seeing how Andrew was crumbling beneath a guilt that shouldn't have been his to bear to make that distinction crystal clear to her. "Uncle Clarence has to live with what he did, whatever he did. I won't let it stop me from being with

Andrew or his family. It doesn't have to be one way or the other."

Her father said, "How did we get such a wise daughter?"

"It might have something to do with the quality of the parents who raised me." Her parents chuckled. She thought of one more thing she wanted their opinion on. "Would it be over-the-top pushy of me if I called a family meeting with his family?"

"Oh, honey," her mother said, "that might lead to a huge clash with them."

"What if I showed up at the breakfast they invited us to this morning? Just went without Andrew?"

"It's not what I would do," her mother hedged.

Her father said, "What are you hoping to get out of going?"

"His mother said that her children don't know how to talk out their problems. They don't know how to pull together when things go wrong. This is an awkward situation and telling them what Andrew said will be painful, but if I share how I feel, maybe it'll help them see that love is always worth the pain. You taught me that, Dad. I'm not ashamed to let anyone see my tears. I love Andrew, and I think it would help them if they see how a Franklin loves."

"Oh, what the hell," her father said, "call a family meeting. They sound like they need one."

Chapter Twenty

LATER THAT DAY, Helene stood in the Barrington living room, the center of attention of three generations of Andrew's family. She'd called Sophie and asked her to gather them and there they all were, looking at her with a myriad of expressions on their faces. Some appeared anxious. Some were impatient. When she'd arrived they'd asked her where Andrew was, and she'd said that she'd tell them all at the same time.

She cleared her throat, took out the note Andrew had written to her, and read it aloud. There was a tense silence when she finished. She put the note back into her pocket and met Sophie's eyes across the room. "I could have gone home, but I believe he'll come back to me, just like he'll come back to you. When he does, I want to make sure that we're ready to support him, because he needs us even if he doesn't know how to ask for help." She sniffed. "There's a number people throw around when they talk about veterans and suicide: twenty-two. It's the believed number of veterans who kill themselves each day. Some say it's more. Some say less. These aren't weak men. They're not cowards. These are our strongest and bravest. They went out to protect us and they came back broken. Andrew doesn't want to talk about what happened to him, but that doesn't mean he doesn't need each of you. Don't make him apologize for taking time to heal. Don't make him relive what he wants to forget. When he comes back, just love him with all your heart. That's what I intend to do."

She faced them, chin held high, eyes full of tears but none shed. For a long moment the only sound was that of Asher and Emily's son fussing. The couple exchanged a look and Asher walked over to Helene. She stood her ground and looked him right in the eye when he stopped in front of her.

"Have you talked to him since he left?"

She shook her head.

He let out a long breath. "Do you have any idea where he is?"

She shook her head again.

"I do love him. We all do. No one wants to see him in pain or, God forbid, hurt himself. He doesn't bring his problems to us or we would help him."

"Have you actually ever told him that? That you love him? That this is a place where he can bring his problems?"

Asher frowned and Andrew's father, Dale, stepped forward. "This is my fault. Kenzi told us how she felt she couldn't be herself here, but I didn't understand that Andrew felt the same way."

"This isn't your fault, Dad," Asher said.

"It is. I told you to be careful around your mother. I told you to take it outside . . ."

Sophie went to stand beside Dale and held his hand. "You did that because you thought it was the best for our family. You thought that's what I needed."

Dale shook his head. "How could I have been so wrong? All I wanted to do was to keep this family together."

Kenzi walked over and laid a hand on her father's arm. "You did, Dad. We're all still here."

"All except Andrew," Dale said in a deep, sad voice.

"He'll be back," Helene said. "I'm here because I'm confident he'll return. Hopefully with less guilt on his shoulders. Less pain. The question is, what will you say when he does? How will you show him that when things matter, the Barringtons pull together?"

"We don't need you to tell us how to talk to our own brother," Asher said.

His wife walked up and put her arm around him. "We could hear her out."

ANDREW SAT ACROSS from Colonel Ahearn on the porch of the man's house on the Marine base in North Carolina. They were both dressed in civilian attire.

"What can I do for you, Marine?"

"I'm here to talk to you about my last mission."

"It was a tragic and unfortunate loss of life. I was sorry to hear that you chose not to reenlist. You had a promising career with the Corps."

"Thank you. Something's been eating at me since that day. I saw the contents of the crate before it burned in the fire. It was nothing more than a pilot seat from a MiG."

"What are you trying to say, Marine?"

"I think you lied when you said we went there to pick up classified equipment. You sent us on a personal errand that cost Marines their lives and then covered it up."

"My intel said different. I don't know what was in that crate, and I don't care. My orders were to retrieve it. Your orders were the same."

"I looked into the mission and it didn't come down from higher than you. This was your personal order. I can prove this and have friends who will hang you if need be."

"Who the hell do you think you're threatening? I could have MPs here and you in the brig before you reached your car."

Andrew stood. "Yeah, that's not going to happen. I don't think you know who you are dealing with. I not only have the resources and the connections to crush you, it would feel really fucking good to do it."

The colonel was on his feet. "Do it. I don't believe you can or you would have."

Andrew went nose to nose with him. "The only thing that has stopped me so far is my concern for the families of the Marines who died, but after some soul-searching, I believe they'd approve of what I'm about to say. You resign today. You leave. I don't care what reason you give. You're done. I don't believe you meant for them to die, but you showed a lack of respect for the lives of all Marines when you sent us in for a trophy. If the MPs come for anyone, it'll be you. I'm giving you one chance to leave with what's left of your honor or everyone will know what happened. If you're still here tomorrow, I won't stop until you're court-martialed and spending time in Leavenworth."

The colonel's face went bright red. "How dare you stand there and threaten me. Get the hell out of my house."

"Gladly," Andrew said, and as he was walking out the door, he stopped. "I was proudly a platoon sergeant, but I have always been and will always be a Barrington. If you don't know the name, you might want to learn it." He left with another look. Andrew held his head high and proud as he walked out. Nothing would bring his friends back, but he had honored them that day. The bastard who had sent them to their deaths would send no one else to theirs.

He was back in the air less than an hour later and in Virginia shortly after that. He walked across the thick green grass between rows and rows of white headstone markers. Every stone was the same, because every man's life was valued the same. There they were all equal, all brothers and sisters, all mourned deeply.

Three stones. Three Marines. Laid to rest side by side in death, as they had been in life. He dropped to one knee, placed one hand on his heart and the other on the stone. "I know what you're thinking, Lofton. If I dragged my feet for one more damn minute you were going to come back and do it yourself. It's done, though. One way or another, I did what I think you would have wanted me to do. I'll make sure your family never wants for anything, and I'll do it in a way they can be proud of. I don't know what that will look like yet, but I know you would have done it for me and mine. I haven't seen Gabrielle since the funeral, but I promise to give all of Giniya's future boyfriends hell for you."

Andrew rose to his feet and sighed. An older man wearing a World War II veteran baseball cap came to stand beside him. "I come here once a year and it never gets easier, but I don't think it's supposed to." He referenced a woman standing outside a car parked behind Andrew's. "That's my daughter. She comes with me now that my wife passed. She doesn't understand what I do here, but you do. When I saw you I remembered my first time. I don't know what you saw or what happened to your friends, but I hope this helps you. What does a Marine do when he comes across a fallen comrade? He picks him up. He carries him if need be. That kind of brotherhood doesn't bow to death. These men are strong enough to carry whatever weight you bear. Give it to them, then honor them by being a good man, husband, and father. A good friend to those who need it. And when you see a man down on his knees never be too busy to stop and help him."

Blinking back emotion, Andrew shook the man's hand and promised to do just that. When he left the cemetery a while later, he drove back to the airport but didn't call Helene. If Ahearn didn't resign, the following day would start an ugly battle that would play out in the courts and probably the media. He wanted to spare her from that.

He made one call home and without bothering with niceties, said, "I need your help."

Dax Marshall answered forcefully, "Whatever you need."

"Your friend, Clay Landon, can he be discrete?"

"If I threaten his life, yes."

"He runs a foundation for Veterans, right?"

"Yes."

"I have three families I want taken care of, but I don't want them to know I'm doing it. Could he do that for me?"

"Absolutely."

"Thanks. I'll send you the information."

"Andrew?"

"Yes."

"There are a lot of people here who care about you."

"I know."

"Helene is running a relationship-building boot camp to prepare them for your return. You'd better marry that girl. She's something else."

Andrew shook his head in bewilderment. "She's what?"

"You'll see when you get back. When will that be?"

"I don't know. There's something I need to handle first."

"You don't have to handle it alone."

"For now I do, but I know you have my back if I need you. I'll try not to get you shot at this time."

"I'd appreciate that."

"I never thanked you for sending Emmitt."

"Not necessary. You're family."

It was an interesting comment from someone who had recently joined the Barringtons, but it rang true. For a long time Andrew had considered his true family to be the men and women he served beside. He was beginning to see that it didn't have to be like that. Like his mother, he had closed himself off. He hadn't been whole even before losing Lofton and the others.

Dax made family sound like a treasured commitment. There was something inspiring about seeing a man who, if his reputation were to be believed, had lived a hard and solitary life until he met Kenzi.

Relationship-building boot camp? I could use it, too.

After hanging up with Dax, Andrew decided to make one more call. "It's Andrew," he said.

"It's Andrew," Helene's mother echoed.

"You can put me on speakerphone."

"Where are you? Are you with Helene?" her father asked.

"No, I haven't spoken to her since this morning after I left her in Boston." He braced himself for a possibly emotional reaction.

"We know," her mother said calmly.

Of course they do. Helene didn't hide things from her family. Wonderful. Ugly. She brought it all to them. Had she told them his secret? Without asking, he knew she hadn't. She was loyal and believed in promises. Although he'd arranged for a plane to take her home, a part of him had known she wouldn't go. "How is she?"

"Confused," Art said in a stern tone. "And she's not alone."

"There's something I need to do before I can be with her."

"Does it involve another woman?" Art asked.

Rose chastised him quickly, "Of course it doesn't. He wouldn't do that."

Art countered, "Rose, let the boy answer."

"No, sir, it doesn't." He took a leap of faith then and

told them exactly what it did involve.

Both of her parents were quiet for several minutes after he finished. In a sympathetic tone Art asked, "Does Helene know this?"

"I told her last night."

Rose asked, "What are you going to do?"

"It depends on what Ahearn does. If he resigns, it's over."

"And if he doesn't?" Art asked.

"I'll expose him and the cover-up. I don't have proof, so it won't be easy, but it's the right thing to do. I can't let him send anyone else to their deaths."

"You didn't want Helene at your side for this?" Rose asked.

Andrew didn't answer at first because he didn't think they'd understand. It wasn't that he didn't trust Helene to take his side. She would, but this was his fight. He couldn't bear for another person to be hurt by it.

"You love her," Art said simply.

"Yes, sir," Andrew said. "More than I know how to express in words. She's the piece of me I didn't even know was missing. When I'm with her, life makes sense. I want you to know that I will dedicate my life to keeping her safe, to finding ways to make her smile, and the causes that are important to her will always be important to me. When this is over, I plan to ask her to marry me, and I'm asking for your blessing."

Art cleared his throat. "We could use a sharpshooter around here."

Andrew chuckled.

Her mother said, "I've always wanted a son, but once you two start having babies you have to get your own place."

Andrew laughed again. There was a simplicity to her parents that lightened the weight he'd carried for so long. They didn't ask him a hundred questions about what he'd been through. They didn't need him to change who he was to be with them. "Will do."

Art interjected, "If you need us, son, we'll fly up to be with you."

He loved that Helene's father not only made that offer, but meant it. *No wonder Helene is so fiercely loyal. Family. They know how to do it right.* "No, but I'll call you tomorrow and update you."

"We would love that," her father said.

"You should call Helene, too," her mother said.

"He will," her father added.

"I know, but she's waiting and all worried," her mother continued.

"Let the boy figure it out himself. He'll do the right thing."

"Ask him what you asked me."

"I'll ask him later."

"You said you really wanted to know so you might as well ask while you have him on the phone."

Andrew broke in, "What do you want to know, Art?"

Her father asked slowly, "Are those guys still watching us from the trees?"

Chapter Twenty-One

>>><<<

A FTER DINNER THE next evening, Helene was reading in the living room with Andrew's parents. Although she hadn't heard from Andrew, she refused to second-guess her decision to wait for him. She wasn't entirely comfortable with staying with his parents yet, but Sophie had insisted, and Helene was beginning to see that the woman could be just as stubborn as she was—in a wonderful, loving way.

Which made it harder and harder to not feel awful about what her uncle had done to this family. To her family as well because no matter how many times Helene told herself she wasn't responsible for what her uncle had done, the guilt lingered. She knew her parents felt the same, even though they didn't talk about it either.

There was a lot to be positive about. The previous evening had started off rocky, but Helene hadn't let it discourage her. She'd considered the worst-case scenario: Andrew didn't come back, and his family threw her out, claiming she'd inappropriately inserted herself into their business. The risk had been worth it and so far it appeared to have paid off. The tension regarding Andrew's return as well as his departure seemed to have lessened. If nothing else, Andrew's family had heard her out. If they repeated their first reception of Andrew then shame on them. She had done all she could.

Well, short of telling them what her family had done to theirs.

Sophie called out, "Asher. Emily. We didn't expect you tonight. Where's Joseph?"

Emily crossed over and gave her mother-in-law a kiss. "We left him with a babysitter."

"Really?" Dale asked as he stood. "And you chose to spend that coveted sanity time with us?" He shook Asher's hand. "Come on in. We're having a quiet night."

Asher took Emily's hand and walked over to sit across from Helene. He took a photo out of his breast pocket and handed it to her. "I have something for you."

It was a holiday photo of five young children, all under the age of ten. Four boys in suits and little Kenzi in a pretty dress and diaper. Helene smiled. The boys had their arms around each other's shoulders and enough devil in their eyes to imply that it wasn't the pose the photographer had requested.

Sitting forward, with his elbows on his knees, Asher said, "Until you made us face it, I didn't realize how far we'd gone from how close we were back then. And, before your speech yesterday, I thought the status quo was set in stone when it doesn't have to be. I tell my employees that you can't achieve something you can't visualize. You have to know what you want, take action to make it a reality, and see every obstacle as surmountable. I want my children to see my siblings and me the way I was in that photo."

Helene looked at the picture briefly, but was saddened by what she knew was missing from it. And why. She turned the photo over and asked herself if she had any business telling this family how to behave when her own family might be the cause of their issues.

Grant and Ian strolled in, joining the mix. "What do you have there?" Grant asked.

Helene passed him the photo. "A photo of my favorite family."

He laughed and showed Ian. "I remember that day. None of you were listening to the poor photographer."

Ian clapped a hand on Grant's shoulder. "You made up for our bad behavior by advising on how upselling certain packages would increase his profits. He loved you."

Asher leaned in. "Do you remember how we blamed the trouble on Lance, and he started to cry?"

"Watch what you share, Asher, I have plenty of stories about you," Lance said as he entered the room with Willa.

Grant chuckled. "One year Asher was convinced Mom and Dad were trying to kill him because he got hurt doing everything they warned him not to do. They would point at something, tell him how dangerous it was, and he'd be on it the second they turned their backs."

"They made it sound too good," Asher said with a shrug and a grin. "See that skateboard, Asher? Whatever you do, don't use it in the kitchen on the marble floor. Who could resist seeing why?"

Emily hugged his side. "Let's hope Joseph doesn't take after you."

"Unless you have more children," Lance interjected. "There were perks to being Asher's little brother. I was never bullied."

Asher flexed his shoulders. "I would have killed anyone who bothered you."

Grant joked, "Ian would have gotten them expelled. He was on every ruling committee there was."

Ian winked at Helene. "Grant would have still advised them on their retirement. He can't help himself."

Everyone laughed. Helene laughed along, but the reality of what she knew stopped her from feeling joy with them. *Is this how Andrew always feels? Riddled with guilt that isn't his, but is unshakeable?*

Kenzi and Dax joined the group. Shrugging off her coat, Kenzi said, "The traffic was horrendous. I'm glad we're not late."

"Late? For what?" Helene asked.

Kenzi looked around as if asking for help. "Impromptu game night?"

Helene hadn't heard anything about it, but she was beginning to feel that something else was going on. Were they there because they felt sorry for her since there had been no word from Andrew? The way they were gathering around her certainly made it seem that way. There was hope for these Barringtons yet.

She was preparing to thank them when her parents walked into the living room. Helene jumped to her feet.

"Mom. Dad. What are you doing here?" She flew across the room to give them each a hug. She'd never been so happy to see them.

After releasing her from a tight bear hug, her father said, "We're here to see you, silly."

Helene wiped away happy tears that poured down her cheeks. "I told you you didn't have to come."

Her mother added, "How could we stay away?"

Helene introduced her parents to Sophie and Dale, then to each of their children. They were soon chatting comfortably. Like Helene, her parents weren't intimidated by the affluence of the Barringtons and that allowed them to be easily accepted into the mix. Her father and Dale got along so well they stepped away from everyone else to talk privately.

She wondered if her parents felt as she did. Part of her was proud of his family. She wished Andrew could have been there to see how well everyone was getting along. She badly wanted to see him right there with them, laughing over childhood stories.

Another part of her felt like she didn't belong there, could never belong there. Even if Andrew returned.

Dale and her father rejoined the group, then Dale glanced down at his phone and said, "Excuse me for a moment. I'll be right back."

ANDREW HAD JUST pulled into the driveway of his parents' home and had texted his father to make sure everyone had arrived. As soon as he'd received news that Ahearn had resigned without fanfare, Andrew had known where he was headed next.

He might never again be the man he'd been before Lofton and the others had died, but if he did this right he would be someone who could look himself in the mirror again. The advice from the older veteran he'd met in the cemetery rang true to him. He would never forget his friends and their loss would always be with him, but it was one he wouldn't let beat him. The guilt had already taken too much from him. He was now determined to put his effort into becoming a good husband, and God willing, a good father. While he was at it, he'd do his best to be a better son and brother. That was how he would honor Lofton, by not only taking care of his friend's family, but his own as well.

His father met him on the steps and handed him a small box. Andrew opened it, revealing an antique ring with a simple round stone. "Art and Rose are inside. They asked me to give this to you. It was his mother's."

Andrew closed the box with a nod and pocketed it.

Dale cleared his throat. "The Franklins seem like good people."

"They are." Andrew met his father's eyes for a long moment. In the past he hadn't been able to look at his father without seeing what Andrew had always considered weakness. It had taken hitting rock bottom for him to view the man before him more kindly. *I don't know why he made the choices he did, but it may be time to forgive him for being fallible . . . human.*

"Your mother and I had a long talk after you left. There's

something I need to tell you—"

"It's okay, Dad."

His father took hold of his forearm. "This has been a wonderful year for our family, but also a rough one. We've had to face some tough truths about who we are. Me especially. I need you to know that I always have been and always will be proud of you. I was wrong about so many things, but I thought I was doing what was best for our family."

Andrew placed his hand over his father's. "I know that, Dad."

"Do you?" Dale asked in a tight voice. "Don't give up on us, Andrew. We need you every bit as much as you've ever needed us."

Andrew thought about how often he'd felt on the outside of his own family, unable to fit no matter how he tried. He could hold onto that feeling or he could embrace the acceptance and loving trust he'd experienced with Helene and her family. His relationship with his father, as well as the rest of his family, was not only a commitment, but also a choice.

He'd told himself he wanted to be a better son and this was his opportunity to test that decision. He could hold onto the past or let it all go and start fresh.

Andrew dropped his arm, breaking that contact with his father, then pulled him in for a tight hug. His father returned the hug with the same intensity. After a final pat to his father's back, Andrew stepped back. "We're good, Dad."

Dale's eyes shone with emotion. "We're good." He took a deep breath. "One more thing. Kenzi told me you went to Aruba to investigate things in your aunt's journal. Did you discover anything?"

Andrew tensed. His family had accepted Helene. What would they think if they knew about her connection to Kent's death? Even though she'd had nothing to do with it, would it change the way they saw her? He refused to give tragedies from the past more power than they already had. "Nothing worth sharing."

His father let out an audible sigh of relief. "I'm glad. Patrice Stanfield was truly a sick woman. She couldn't bear the idea of your mother being happy and did everything she could to undermine it. As awful as it sounds, I was relieved when I heard she was dead. She can't hurt us anymore."

The depth of the pain in Dale's eyes was unsettling. How far had his aunt gone to hurt his parents? He remembered what Helene had once said, "Then maybe your aunt killed them . . ." What was his aunt's tie to Stiles and to Kent's death? Would Patrice Stanfield have gone as far as to hurt one of her sister's children? Andrew was about to ask his father what exactly his aunt was capable of when the front door opened.

Asher stepped out onto the top step. "Are we doing this or what?"

Dale turned and said, "Asher—"

Asher walked down to stand beside Andrew. "Get your ass in there, Andrew, and propose before Helene realizes how fucked up we all are and runs back to Florida. This family needs her."

"We *are* a sorry bunch," Andrew said and gave Asher a hard pat on the arm.

Asher returned the gesture. "But we pick good women."

Andrew glanced in the direction of the living room where he guessed the family and Helene were gathered. "Yes, we do." He looked at Asher again. "Emily has almost brought you around to being likable."

"Almost, huh?" Asher asked. "Be nice or I'll tell Helene you hurt my feelings. I bet she'd make you apologize."

"Oh, if I'm going to apologize anyway, then it should be for something I actually did, like put my foot up your ass—"

"Enough," Dale said with a laugh and two hands in the air as he called for a truce. "Let's go add another member to our family."

Andrew and Asher exchanged a look and, for the first time in a very long time, Andrew didn't feel as if they were on opposing sides. *We can do better than we've done. We will do better.* Shoulder to shoulder with his brother, he walked into his parents' home. Someday he'd tell Asher about Lofton and Ahearn, but it could wait.

Chapter Twenty-Two

FRESH FROM A conversation with Sophie about key terms to use when wooing donations from the Boston elite, Helene turned to check if her parents were still enjoying themselves. They were smiling and talking comfortably with Ian and Grant. She overhead her mother describing the day-to-day routine of running the rescue and was pleased at how genuinely interested Andrew's brothers appeared. The Barringtons might have complicated relationships with each other, but they weren't snobs. Their warm welcome of her parents made her want to hug each and every one of them.

A sudden silence fell over the room, and Helene glanced over her shoulder toward the hallway. Her stomach did a nervous flip when she saw Andrew crossing the room toward her. In what felt like slow motion she walked toward him until they met in the middle of the room.

Everyone and everything else faded away until it was just the two of them. Neither spoke at first. Worry mixed with love as Helene searched his face. "You're back."

"I'm sorry I left the way I did. There was something I had to do," he said.

A hundred questions flew to the tip of her tongue, but she voiced only one. "And it's done?"

"Yes."

When she'd first met him she would have worried what that simple answer was hiding, but she trusted Andrew in a way that didn't require the details. He'd tell her when he was ready. What mattered more to her was that he'd said he wouldn't come back until he could give her what she gave him. That had to mean what she hoped it did. She searched his face but it was carefully neutral.

"I'm back for good."

Her knees went weak, but she steadied herself. "That sounds like a very long time."

"I sure as hell hope so." He dropped to one knee and took out the ring box Art had brought from Florida. "Marry me, Helene."

Love like she'd never imagined filled her when she realized the ring was her grandmother's. She glanced around at the smiling faces of his family and hers. She took the ring and held it up, turning it as if she were debating something within herself. She certainly wasn't. Every cell in her wanted to scream yes, but she needed to talk to him first. She looked around and knew she couldn't say no in front of his family, but that didn't mean that they didn't need to talk. For the moment, she decided to keep it light. "I suppose I could consider it."

He stood and pulled her to him with a laugh. "*Consider* it?"

Her hands went to his shoulders and she gave him a

cheeky smile. "Maybe if you say you love me it'll help me make up my mind."

"You want to know how I feel?" He lifted her off her feet so she was smiling down at him. "When we met I was sure I'd never feel anything again, then you steamrolled right into my heart, fearless and loyal. I love you so much I can't think straight."

With the ring still in one hand, she did her best to steady herself as he swung her around. Her heart was thudding wildly. "That does sound promising."

He slid her down his front and growled. "Maybe this will make up your mind." The passionate kiss he gave her left her breathless and sagging against him.

With a laugh and a prayer, she slid the ring on her finger. Something this good had to work out. It couldn't crumble in the face of the truth. "I love you, too, Mr. Muscles."

"Mr. Muscles," Asher parroted with a laugh.

"It's cute," his wife said warmly.

"And hard to live down," Andrew's youngest brother, Lance, added cheerfully.

"I don't think he cares right now," Ian said dryly.

Andrew kissed Helene again lightly, causing her to almost forget that they were very much the center of attention. She wrapped her arms around his neck, and after the kiss broke off she buried her face in his chest. They'd come into each other's lives for a reason. She believed that. They might not know the answers, but together they would find them. With love, anything was possible.

"Congratulations," Art said loudly.

Helene raised her head, looked down at the ring on her left hand, and said, "It's perfect." Then she wagged a finger at her parents. "I can't believe you two knew and didn't say anything."

"If you had been sad it would have been more difficult, but you knew he was coming back." Her mother was all smiles, snuggling against her father's side. "We're so happy for you, honey."

Holding hands, Sophie and Dale said, "We are, too."

Helene looked up at Andrew and said a truth she could share. "I never doubted that you'd come back because I know you." She tapped his heart, then his temple. "In here and in here. You're a good man and I love you, all of you."

He hugged her closer. "I don't know if I deserve the faith you have in me, but I'll spend the rest of my life trying to."

They were about to kiss again when Sophie asked, "So who would like coffee?"

THE EVENING AT his parents' was passing too quickly and that in itself was a novel feeling for Andrew. He knew he'd never tire of watching Helene banter with his brothers and swap stories with Kenzi and his sisters-in-law. More than once he caught his parents nod in approval and understood.

Every once in a while, though, he caught Helene looking away during a conversation and his gut clenched. He wanted the evening to be euphoric for both of them, and although she was happy there was something holding her back.

Knowing what it was didn't make it easier. He could compare it to why he would never tell Gabrielle how her husband had died, but it wasn't the same.

He tried to tell himself that he was wrong about what was bothering Helene, but he overheard Kenzi asking her for details about how they'd met and Helene looked torn and evasive again. *Am I willing to ask the woman I love to spend a lifetime lying to my family because I'm not sure they can handle the truth?*

Is that fair to her?

To them?

He looked over at his mother and remembered what Dax had said about her not being as fragile as everyone thought. Not telling her would fit into the pattern his family was comfortable with, but wasn't that what had stood in the way of them being close?

Andrew walked over and asked Helene to step into the other room with him for a moment. She nodded without asking him why as if she knew that he knew what was bothering her.

In the quiet of his father's study, he pulled her into his arms and kissed her gently before cupping her face with his hands. "You know what your uncle did is not a burden you should carry. You weren't there, you didn't know, and his sins are not yours."

She blinked back tears. "I know and I didn't think about it at all when you were gone. All I focused on then was you coming back and how much I wanted everything to be perfect when you did. And you're here. Everything *is* perfect. Unless I open my mouth and ruin it—"

"I get it. Believe me, I get it." He buried his face in her

hair.

"My parents won't say anything if we don't, but I can see that this will weigh on my parents, too. We're not a family that keeps secrets."

Andrew raised his head. "I couldn't be with you until I confronted Ahearn and you helped me see that. He resigned this morning. Your love gave me the strength to do what Lofton would have wanted for his family. There would be no gain in telling Gabrielle or the others, but now their memories have been honored in the way they needed to be. You did that."

She searched his face. "So, maybe we can do something but I need to keep it inside."

"No, the more I think about how my father lost his career around the same time as my brother dying, the more I believe that secrets are what is wrong with my family. The longer we keep denying that something happened, the more it holds us hostage. It's time to set my family free. I'll tell them."

Helene shook her head and laid a hand on his chest. "No. *We'll* tell them."

"Yes, *we* will." He smiled, pleased but not surprised by her correction. No matter what had happened in the past or what the future would bring, they had each other. He laced his fingers with hers and his heart pounded in his chest with love for her. She was a light the demons within him recoiled from and when he looked into her eyes he believed in possibilities again. Finding out that his brother's death hadn't been accidental might shake his family up, but they would survive and come out stronger. He'd made sure of it. "Let's do it."

All eyes were on them when they walked back into the living room hand in hand. He said, "There's something I need to tell you." Andrew squared his shoulders. He met Art's eyes across the room. As if understanding what was about to happen, Art put his arm around his wife and pulled her close.

Helene said, "Thank you for welcoming me into your family. Sophie, Dale, I couldn't have asked for a nicer reception. There's something, though, that you need to know."

Still holding her hand, Andrew added, "The truth is ugly, but you deserve to hear it."

"My uncle told us to stay quiet because he was afraid. The advice of a coward is simply that." She looked up at Andrew with a teary smile. "We won't be held hostage by the lies of others."

Her mother rushed to her side. "Oh, Lenny."

Art followed his wife and the four stood together. "I'm proud of you."

Helene gave Andrew one last look then said, "My uncle is Clarence Stiles, and according to him, the death of your youngest son, Kent, was not an accident. I don't know how, but my uncle was involved in whatever happened."

"What?" Sophie asked, looking confused. Her mouth opened and closed a few times but no further words came out.

"What do you mean not an accident?" Asher stormed.

"Involved how?" Dale asked hoarsely.

Andrew raised a hand and said, "The most important thing you need to know is that neither Helene nor her parents had anything to do with it."

"I don't understand," Kenzi said slowly. "Are you suggesting Kent didn't die at childbirth?" Dax put a support arm around her.

When Andrew spoke next it was with calm authority. "Not according to what we were told by her uncle."

"I'm sure you misunderstood," Ian said firmly, looking over at his mother. "This isn't something we should discuss now."

Sophie walked over to stand in front of Helene and Andrew. "No. I need to know. Kent was alive when he was born, wasn't he?" She gripped Helene's arm.

Helene looked at Andrew before answering. "It sounded that way. My uncle only said that his death wasn't an accident. It was deliberate."

Grant strode over. "This doesn't make any sense. Why would anyone do such a thing? It's pure evil."

Sophie swayed on her feet. "I think I know." She steadied herself by holding onto Helene's arm. "But no. She wouldn't go that far."

Andrew laid his hand over his mother's. In the past he would have spared her the full reality, but the truth might be what she needed. "She knew about it. It was her journal that led us to Aruba. It is full of phone numbers and names of people who were there when Kent died. I wish I could tell you that she had nothing to do with it, but I believe she did."

Sophie brought a hand to her mouth. Dale went to her side in support. "Your sister was crazy, Sophie. She might have written all of that down after the fact. You know how obsessed she was with you."

Sophie released Helene's arm and sat down heavily. "I knew it. I knew the clinic lied to us about when Kent died. I remembered holding him in my arms, but they said I had imagined it. They said I was crazy." Dale sat beside her. "Kent wasn't born dead. He was alive." She looked around blindly, lost in memories. "I didn't have a breakdown; I knew the truth. I knew someone had taken my baby and I was right. All that time I wasn't crazy; I was right."

Kenzi went to her mother and took both of her hands in hers, nodding and looking her mother in the eye. "You're not crazy, Mom. I've always felt him with me."

Andrew's father swayed beside his wife. "The doctors said . . . Oh, my God." His voice faded off.

With tears pouring down her cheeks, Sophie said, "Kent is still alive. Someone has him."

Andrew exchanged a look with Helene. They both shook their heads. Andrew said, "I'm sorry, Mom."

Sophie looked to Helene's parents. "You have to know something else. Where is my son?"

Rose started crying right along with Sophie. "I'm so sorry, Sophie. I would tell you if I knew anything. My brother never spoke to me about it."

Sophie wiped her tears away and took several deep breaths. She stood and faced Helene. "You said your uncle was involved? Where is he? I want to talk to him."

Although it was heartbreaking to see his mother so upset, she was handling it better than he thought. Shock had put her into denial, but that would pass. "When we uncovered the truth he bolted, and we don't know where he is."

Sophie looked around at everyone and said, "We need to find Kent."

Ian went to her side. "Mom, we know where he is. We buried him."

"That is not my son," Sophie said angrily. "My son is not dead."

There was a steel in her tone that he hadn't heard before. It made him want her to be right. This was ugly. It was dark, uncharted territory . . . territory where his family usually failed. Would it destroy them or could they do what Helene's family did and pull together rather than apart? It would have been easy enough to tell his mother she was wrong and she would have to come to accept that Kent was dead, but wasn't that what everyone had done when it happened? Wasn't that how his family had gotten to this place? Change would require someone being brave enough to believe. Andrew looked down at Helene and knew he could be that man. "If Mom thinks Kent is alive, then we look for him."

Helene hugged Andrew's side and smiled through tears. "I'm in."

Ever the voice of reason, Grant said, "If the man who was responsible said Kent is dead, the chance that he's not is miniscule."

Andrew threw both of his hands up in the air. "I don't

need a fucking statistical probability of success. If Mom says he's alive, he is." He looked across to his father. "Did you run a blood test on the baby you buried?"

Dale shook his head. His expression was blank from shock. "I don't think so. It's not something you ask for when you're picking out your baby's casket."

Sophie grabbed one of Andrew's hands and one of Kenzi's. "Thank you for believing me." She looked around to each of her other children and Dale. "Kent is alive. Find him."

Helene glanced at Andrew. "Do you still have that card? The black one you said that woman gave you? Didn't you say she sounded like she knew things?"

Andrew hunted through his wallet for the card then took it out and frowned. "I've called it several times, but she doesn't answer. I don't know who she is."

Lance stepped forward. "I had a black card like that. A woman gave it to me after telling me to read Patrice's journal."

Asher walked over and pulled out a matching card. "Her name is Alethea Niacharos. I hired her to help me solve the cause of the fire at Emily's museum. Dominic warned me that if I invited her she would dig around, but no one else can do what she does. Did she say she thought Kent was alive?"

"She said she's one step ahead of us on this. But I've called that number and no one answered," Andrew said impatiently.

Sophie took the card out of Andrew's hand. "She'll answer me."

Helene slipped beneath Andrew's arm. She laid a hand across his chest. "I hope telling her was the right thing to do."

"It was." Andrew held her to him and kissed her forehead. His mother strode out of the room with the card in hand. Kenzi went with her. Dale raced after both of them, leaving the rest standing in stunned silence.

Asher took out his phone.

Ian nodded at it. "Who are you calling?"

"Dominic Corisi. Alethea will answer Mom's call."

"Do you think that's wise?" Grant asked. "Maybe we should talk to her first."

"Who? Mom or the Niacharos woman?" Ian asked.

Asher paused before dialing. "This whole situation is batshit crazy to me, but Andrew is right. This isn't about Kent as much as it is about Mom. If someone told me that Joseph was dead and I thought he wasn't—" His voice broke.

Emily hugged his side. "Dead or alive, I would need to know. I would need to see the proof."

Grant said, "Before you make that call, why don't we hear everything Andrew knows?"

With that, they all turned toward Andrew and Helene. Andrew told most of the story but Helene added what she could. Her parents gently contributed even though they didn't reveal anything new.

At the end, Helene said, "I can't express how sorry I am that a member of my family—"

Rose touched her daughter's arm. "Our family."

Andrew said firmly, "My family now, as well. The weight of what he did isn't yours to carry, but if you do, you won't carry it alone."

Rose pulled on Andrew's arm so he bent and then she kissed his cheek. "Thank you."

Andrew looked around at his siblings. "They say that you don't know who you are until the bullets start flying for real. Well, they're fucking flying now. So what are you going to do?"

Asher held up his phone. "I'm making a call. I don't believe that Kent is alive, but if Mom does, I agree that we need to do everything we can to find out what happened to him."

"We'll need a plan," Ian said.

Asher waved his phone. "The plan is to find out what happened."

"If we open this door and it leaks out it'll be a feeding frenzy for the news," Ian warned. He turned to Andrew and Helene. "You say you don't know who Stiles was afraid of but that we could all be in danger from them. I'd say that requires a more thoughtful approach."

Finally breaking his silence, Dax said, "I have some people in Aruba who are looking into this already."

Asher nodded. "Good. Andrew, do you think you could find Stiles?"

Andrew glanced down at Helene. The answer was right there in her eyes. "I know *we* can." He raised her hand and kissed it.

Helene sniffed and nodded. "Together."

Grant stepped forward and said, "No, I'll find him. A money trail never gets cold. Nobody does something for nothing." He took the card from Asher and said, "If Kent is out there, I'll find him. If that search starts with Clarence Stiles, that's where I'll begin." He looked across at Ian. "I'll do it discretely, but I'll keep you all in the loop."

Asher took his wife's hand in his, then walked over and placed his other on Andrew's shoulder. "I'm here and every resource I have is yours to use. No one stands alone in this family. No one ever will again."

One by one the rest of them nodded.

In the silence that followed, Asher looked across at Helene and her parents and said, "You are part of this family now, Helene. You, and your parents. You stood by Andrew and by us and nothing we discover will change that."

Helene hugged Andrew's side. His love for her exceeded what he would ever be able to express in words. Whatever the future held for them, no matter what truth was revealed, they would survive if they held to each other as tightly as they did in that moment.

Helene's relationship boot camp rivaled the one that had earned Andrew the title of Marine, and it had changed him just as deeply. He knew now that when he visited Lofton's grave next year, he would report that he was keeping up his end of the bargain. He would be the son, brother, husband who would honor his friend's memory.

Epilogue

✦❯❯❯❯❮❮❮❮✦

THREE WEEKS LATER, Helene and Andrew were standing outside the physiological sciences building at the University of Florida after concluding a guided tour of the entire campus. Although Andrew had encouraged Helene to follow her dream of going into veterinary medicine, it still all felt so unreal. She looked down at the ring on her finger then over to the man at her side. He was dressed in a casual pair of slacks and a white collared shirt, which should have made him blend in, but a man of his impressive physical build and his television-worthy features would always stand out in a crowd. Young women literally stopped, smacked their friends, and drooled over him before moving on. If Helene were the type to be threatened by competition she would have worried, but Andrew didn't spare any of them a single look. "I love you," Helene said spontaneously.

"I know," he said cheekily, then grinned. "We're here to decide on a college. Focus."

She gave him a light hip check. "Oh, I'll focus later . . . if you're lucky."

He laughed and kissed her briefly. "Seriously, what did

you think?"

Helene let out a slow breath. "It's perfect. I can do my undergrad courses online and at satellite campuses. We could make this work, but . . ."

"But?" He turned, running his hands up and down her arms lightly. "You tell me what's standing in your way, and I'll remove that obstacle."

He meant it, but she still worried. "It's just with everything that is going on with your family, I hate to tie you to Florida. If they uncover anything, they'll need you in Boston."

"Us. They'll need us. And we can be there in a few hours by plane. What else is worrying you?"

She wanted to say nothing, but the strength of her bond to Andrew was their honesty with each other. "I know you enjoying working at the rescue—"

"I do. After the Marines, I didn't think I'd have a purpose again, but the rescue gave that to me." His smile turned nostalgic. "Thank you for pushing me to invite Gabriella and Giniya. They enjoyed the visit, and I needed to see them." He cocked his head to one side and said, "How do you always know what I need before I do?"

Because I see the beauty of you, inside and out. That's why I need to make sure this is right for you, too. "I'm brilliant like that, I guess." She took a moment to simply bask in how good it felt to be with him then returned to a topic she knew needed to be addressed. "Are you sure you're okay with living at my parents' house?"

He rubbed his chin thoughtfully. "Although I love your

parents, staying with them long-term won't be ideal." A slow, self-satisfied grin spread across his face. "Which is why I purchased two hundred acres of land abutting the rescue. It'll give the rescue room to expand, and we can build our own place."

Slack-jawed in wondrous awe, Helene asked, "How did you manage that? I wasn't aware it was even for sale."

Andrew shrugged. "I told Asher what I wanted, and he made it happen. He said everyone has a price. I let him negotiate it, and Grant practically came in his pants while listing the tax benefits of investing in the rescue. If you go to school here, ask Grant to pull money from my trust fund to set up a donation to the college. He'll follow you around like a happy puppy for days."

"He's not that bad and you know it," Helene chastised softly, went on her tiptoes, and between light kisses said, "He likes numbers because they make sense to him, and when he talks money it's his way of showing you that he cares. Be nice to him."

Andrew laughed. "I'll try."

After a short pause, Helene asked, "Has he said anything? About—my uncle?"

Pulling Helene to his chest, Andrew sighed. "Not yet, but he won't until he has something solid."

"Nothing new from that woman, Alethea?"

Andrew shook his head. "She said this is a complicated one because so much of it happened long ago and off the grid. People didn't email or text back then so the trails are harder to trace. She's working with Grant, though. She thinks we should exhume Kent's body and do a DNA test, but we haven't brought that option to my parents yet. So far my mother is handling this better than anyone would have expected. We don't want to upset her more."

Sophie was stronger than her sons gave her credit for, but Helene didn't push. She merely nodded and hugged Andrew.

"Excuse me," a deep male voice said from beside them. "Mr. Barrington?"

"Yes?" Andrew turned toward the voice. It didn't bother Helene in the least that so far every faculty member they'd met had been more interested in meeting Andrew than her. The Barrington name carried weight, and Andrew took their adoration in stride. Seeing him remain humble where other men would have become egomaniacs made her love him even more.

"My name is Seth Kidnigh. I'm an adjunct professor, specializing in toxicology."

Andrew shook his hand then introduced Helene. "Nice to meet you."

"When I heard you were visiting the university I mentioned it to a friend of mine in New Mexico. He and I go way back. We went to grade school together. Traveled around the world together before finally losing touch when we both married. That happens. Children and work keep a person busy. You look up and twenty years have gone by."

"I'm sure it does." Andrew nodded and glanced at Helene as if seeking assistance.

Helene held back a chuckle. "What did your friend say?"

The man ran his hands through what was left of his thinning blond hair. "We spoke briefly about your new affiliation with Free Again Rescue and Sanctuary and their history of reintegrating exotic animals back into the wild. He is a large animal veterinarian who specializes in equine medicine but does pro bono work for animal protection groups."

"And?" Helene prompted.

"A private owner was recently caught trying to sell a four-year-old female African elephant for a million dollars. The mother reportedly died in the owner's care and the baby stopped eating. The owner decided to sell her off before she became too sick and lost all value. Local rescues have stepped forward, as well as several zoos, to offer permanent placement for the baby, but my friend has convinced the agency that currently has her to give him a chance to arrange for her to return to Africa. It's an expensive endeavor, but the Free Again Rescue and Sanctuary has done it before and has the contacts."

Not too much shook Helene's confidence, but a memory of the elephant she'd loved and failed to save rattled her. She blinked several times, telling herself she couldn't let her own fears stand in the way of that elephant having a chance to live the life she'd been born to.

She looked up and realized that her reaction had not been lost on Andrew. He raised her hand to his lips and kissed her fingers. "I know what you're thinking, Lenny, and I swear to you we will do everything we can to make sure she is protected. This time you'll be able to go with her to make sure she settles in. Love is always worth it. Isn't that what you say? That little baby needs you."

Helene's eyes filled with tears, but they were happy ones. She threw her arms around his neck. "She needs you, too. Just like I do." Then she kissed him with all the love bursting within her.

The professor cleared his throat. "I'll go into the café and give you time to discuss it."

Although Helene heard him, she gave herself over to the passion of Andrew's kiss. In a few minutes, she and Andrew would hunt down that professor. They'd likely conference call her parents.

In a few minutes.

But right now, Mr. Muscles is setting me on fire.

And I say, "Let it burn . . ."

THE END

Want to keep reading? Sign up here for my newsletter to be notified of the next release:

forms.aweber.com/form/58/1378607658.htm

Or check on my website at www.ruthcardello.com

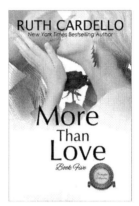

Wondering if you missed one?
Here is my billionaire world at a glance:

45132624R00148

Made in the USA
San Bernardino, CA
25 July 2019